THE HOBBIT™

THE DESOLATION OF SMAUG

OFFICIAL MOVIE GUIDE

THE HOBBIT™

THE DESOLATION OF SMAUG

OFFICIAL
MOVIE GUIDE

BRIAN SIBLEY

HarperCollins*Publishers*

HarperCollins*Publishers*
77–85 Fulham Palace Road,
Hammersmith, London W6 8JB
www.tolkien.co.uk

Published by HarperCollins*Publishers* 2013
1

Photographs: Todd Eyre, James Fisher, Nels Israelson,
Grant Maiden, Mark Pokorny & Steve Unwin; Press
Association (page 12 & 13, bottom); Hagen Hopkins/
Getty Images (page 13, top, page 14, both); Rex Features
(page 15)

Editor: Chris Smith
Cover design: Stuart Bache
Layout design: Terence Caven
Production: Kathy Turtle

A catalogue record for this book
is available from the British Library

ISBN 978 0 00 746447 0
ISBN 978 0 00 752548 5 (Collector's Hardback Edition)

Printed and bound in Italy

**Visit www.tolkien.co.uk for news and
exclusive offers!**

If you have a smartphone, scan this QR code to take you directly
to the Tolkien website. You can download a free QR code reader
from your app store.

CONTENTS

Prologue:

MR BAGGINS,
THE UNEXPECTED HOBBIT

JUST THREE PARAGRAPHS INTO WRITING *THE HOBBIT*, J.R.R. TOLKIEN, HAVING DESCRIBED BAG END, INTRODUCES HIS READERS TO THE BAGGINS FAMILY WHO HAVE LIVED THERE 'FOR TIME OUT OF MIND'. HE TELLS US THAT THEY WERE CONSIDERED RESPECTABLE BECAUSE 'THEY NEVER HAD ANY ADVENTURES OR DID ANYTHING UNEXPECTED' BUT THAT THE TALE WE ARE ABOUT TO READ CONCERNS A BAGGINS WHO 'HAD AN ADVENTURE, AND FOUND HIMSELF DOING AND SAYING THINGS ALTOGETHER UNEXPECTED'.

That is why, for seventy-five years, people of all ages have found themselves caught up in this tale of an unlikely adventurer. For Peter Jackson, Bilbo is both the key to his latest movie trilogy and the link to his previous series of films, *The Lord of the Rings*: 'The Bilbo Baggins that we meet in *The Fellowship of the Ring*, played wonderfully by Ian Holm, is rather eccentric and is treated with suspicion by the rest of the village. There are rumours of great treasure being tucked away in Bag End and tall tales about his having been to extraordinary places and having seen curious things, all of which earmark him as being decidedly odd and peculiar. So, that's the Bilbo that we see at the beginning of *Rings*, but at the beginning of *The Hobbit* he is not like that at all.'

As Peter reflects, the Bilbo encountered in the first few pages of Tolkien's book, and in the opening scenes of *An Unexpected Journey*, is not just a hobbit, but a Baggins, through and through: 'They are insular, small country village people,' says the filmmaker, 'folk who like their comfort and their food and strongly dislike anything that disrupts their world. As a result, they tend to treat strangers – especially wandering Wizards – with great suspicion. Young Bilbo Baggins is a very conservative fellow with no intention of ever leaving his house or his beloved Hobbiton in The Shire. So the worst thing that could happen to him – *I mean the very last thing in the world that he would ever want* – would be to find himself suddenly whisked off into the middle of a dangerous adventure.'

But that, of course, is exactly what happens. 'Which is why the real story of *The Hobbit*,' says Peter, 'is seeing how Bilbo, now played by Martin

Freeman as an innocent, home-loving, safety-conscious hobbit, copes with the twists and turns of that adventure as it unfolds; and, in the process, is fundamentally changed by the experience and begins his transformation into the Bilbo who we meet, sixty years later, in *The Lord of the Rings*.'

But transformations can, sometimes, be slow and painful. At the end of *An Unexpected Journey* – having survived encounters with Trolls, Stone Giants and Goblins, a confrontation with Gollum, an attack by Orcs and Wargs and an airborne rescue by giant Eagles – Bilbo gazes across a vast expanse of, as yet, unexplored wilderness towards the Dragon-occupied Lonely Mountain and says, 'I do believe the worst is behind us.'

However, by that time – having more than a hint of what is still to come – *we* know, without a shadow of a doubt, that Mr Baggins could not be more mistaken…

OPPOSITE: **Director Peter Jackson and Martin Freeman consider Bilbo's next move.** ABOVE: **Things get serious for Bilbo when he enters the spider-filled Mirkwood forest.** RIGHT: **Martin shows his stunt double how to act when in the grip of a very large spider, as Peter looks on.** OVERLEAF: **The Company of Thorin Oakenshield.**

A LONG-EXPECTED PREMIERE

IT IS DECEMBER 2012 AND, FOR THE SECOND TIME IN LESS THAN A DECADE, WELLINGTON, NEW ZEALAND, IS UNDERGOING A MAJOR TRANSFORMATION AS THE CITY PREPARES TO HOST THE WORLD PREMIERE OF *THE HOBBIT: AN UNEXPECTED JOURNEY.* 'WELLINGTON SITS AT THE VERY HEART OF NEW ZEALAND'S INNOVATIVE AND THRIVING FILM INDUSTRY,' SAYS MAYOR CELIA WADE-BROWN. 'IT'S ALSO THE CITY THAT HAS BEEN INTEGRAL IN BRINGING THE FANTASY WORLD OF J.R.R. TOLKIEN TO LIFE ON THE BIG SCREEN. SO, FOR A WEEK AROUND THE PREMIERE, WELLINGTON WILL BE KNOWN AS THE MIDDLE OF MIDDLE-EARTH.'

Travellers from London and Los Angeles get their first glimpse of the extent to which hobbit-mania is gripping the world's southernmost capital on arriving at Air New Zealand's departure desks, decorated with pictures of hobbit legs and feet as if they were the lower halves of the check-in personnel!

Then it's time to board the airline's Boeing 777-300 adorned with giant images of Bilbo, Gandalf and the Dwarves that, at 830 square metres, is the largest ever graphic to be applied to an aircraft. On world premiere day, the plane will fly low over the cheering crowds; but for the actors returning to Wellington for the big day (and fellow premium cabin passengers) it's time to settle back, consult their menus shaped like the round green door to Bag End and open their amenity kits containing an eye-mask printed with the famous notice from Bilbo's gate – 'STRICTLY NO ADMITTANCE Except on party business' – and a pair of flight-socks with hairy hobbit feet design.

Surprisingly, the screening of the flight-safety video is not received with the usual indifference. On the contrary, the sight of an Elf-eared Air New Zealand air hostess standing at a circular plane door instantly grabs the travellers' attention. And this unlikely opening is but a prelude to a witty presentation on the use of seat belts, life

OPPOSITE: **Air New Zealand's special** *Hobbit* **Boeing 777-300 arrives at Wellington airport after a low fly-by over the city.** ABOVE: **Visitors at the airport would be greeted by a giant Gollum hunting for 'fisheses'.** BELOW: **The public is protected from Weta's life-size, and very lifelike, sculptures of the three Trolls as they wait for the red carpet parade to begin.**

jackets and oxygen masks demonstrated by Wizards, hobbits, Dwarves, Elves and Orcs, not to mention Gollum and Peter Jackson. The film doesn't merely capture the imaginations of Air New Zealand passengers, it goes viral on YouTube, delighting millions of fans the world over. At the time of going to press, it has received over 10.5 million views.

Upon arrival, the usually tiresome ordeal of collecting luggage is, on this occasion, decidedly less stressful, since the normally arduous process has been enlivened through the creation of a *Hobbit*-themed luggage carousel for Wellington Airport. Cases, holdalls and backpacks emerge

from Bilbo's front door and trundle along past the windows of Bag End, through which can be glimpsed Bilbo and his Dwarf guests.

For the 2003 premiere of *The Lord of the Rings: The Return of the King*, Weta Workshop created a giant figure of Gollum who could be seen reaching up over the top of the airport building in search of his 'precious'. Nine years later, Weta have built another gigantic Gollum sculpture, only this time suspended inside the lounge and grabbing at a school of passing 'fisheses'.

Weta also helped Bilbo, Thorin and Company take up residence on one of Wellington's most prominent waterfront buildings: the headquarters of New Zealand Post, who will be issuing *Hobbit*-related commemorative stamps and legal tender. A procession of fourteen silhouettes (the tallest standing at six metres and each weighing in at around 300kg) parade across the fifth-floor baluster of the New Zealand Post House building, dramatically back-lit so they can be seen, 24/7, from many vantage points around the city.

Yet another larger-than-life figure is the nine-metre-tall Gandalf, towering over the entrance to the Embassy Theatre and shown placing the 'secret mark' on the door of Bag End, which, as Production Designer Dan Hannah notes, 'Really was the start of the unexpected journey'. There has been technological wizardry going on inside the cinema with a major audio re-fit featuring thirty-six speakers (twenty-eight around the walls and eight overhead) to surround *The Hobbit*'s first audience with all-immersive sound.

LEFT: **James Nesbitt and Evangeline Lilly pose together for photographs.** ABOVE: **Peter emerges from Bag End.** OPPOSITE: **After being introduced by Peter, some of the main cast, including Jed Brophy, Dean O'Gorman, Aidan Turner, Adam Brown, Andy Serkis, Cate Blanchett, Hugo Weaving, Elijah Wood and John Callen, are welcomed by the huge audience of fans.**

Residents and visitors alike have been able to chart the coming premiere, minute by minute, on a Countdown Clock outside the Embassy, although some may be feeling a little unsettled by the recent media revelation that Peter Jackson is still editing the film and has gone on record as saying: 'It's due to be completed literally two days before the premiere – *hopefully*!'

Meanwhile, in the spirit of such hopefulness, and as, in Peter's words, 'a great many sleep-deprived people' are 'working round the clock to get the film finished', Wellington's streets are decked with an ever-increasing proliferation of flags, banners and giant billboards. One of the most startling transformations has been carried out by advertising consultants, ClemengerBBDO, in wrapping their city-centre office building with a fantastical two-storey-high mural depicting Wellington landmarks in the form of a mountain-top citadel standing in a Middle-earthy landscape of rolling plains, cascading waterfalls and soaring peaks. 'At a typical movie premiere,' said Andrew Holt, Clemenger's Executive Creative Director, 'they bring the film to a city, but we thought Wellington doesn't do typical,

so let's do something that puts the city in the middle of Middle-earth.'

Eager followers of the *Hobbit* enterprise – more than 15,000 of them over five days – have been exploring the *Hobbit* Artisan Market in the city's Waitangi Park where the arts-and-crafts people responsible for many of the specially made props created for the film have their wares on display – fabrics, weapons, jewellery – and where there are *Hobbit* food stalls, demonstrations of prosthetic make-up and competitions to find the best Gollum impersonators! In the evenings, giant screens are offering free showings of *The Lord of the Rings* movie trilogy.

On 27 November, 1,500 people begin the final preparations for the following day's premiere: signage, staging, seating and barriers are erected and a 500-metre-long red carpet is rolled out through Courtenay Place to the door of the Embassy. Although there are still twenty-four hours before the stars and guests begin walking that carpet, crowds of fans from all over the world are already gathering. Eager to be part of the big day, they pitch tents and use sleeping bags to reserve themselves coveted front-line positions.

November 28 dawns bright and clear with mounting excitement among the growing crowd. 'It's pretty humbling,' says Peter Jackson, 'on one level I just think we are making a piece of entertainment, but there is this show of support for what we are doing and I am very, very grateful for that.'

Before a packed audience in the national museum, Te Papa, the director and his cast meet the world's press. 'It is,' jokes Barry Humphries, 'the smallest press conference I've ever attended!' Cate Blanchett confesses that there was one point in the film when she had to cover her eyes. When? The moment when the goitre on Barry Humphries' Goblin King starts flopping around. 'It was,' Cate says, 'one of the most horrifying images!'

Back on Courtenay Place, jovial *Hobbit* 'extras' entertain the cheering throng – thousands of whom are wearing Gandalf hats – patiently awaiting the stars, who are making slow progress as they repeatedly stop to sign autographs.

Former inhabitants of Middle-earth mingle with current residents: sometime Gimli, bearded John Rhys-Davies, is there, as is Hugo Weaving who – unlikely though it might seem for an Elf Lord – also has a beard. Cate Blanchett is stunning in red, while Sylvester McCoy wears a suit eccentrically patterned with stars and moons, appropriate, perhaps, for both a Wizard and a past time-travelling Doctor Who. Also present are Evangeline Lilly, whose character, Tauriel, will not be seen until *The Hobbit: The Desolation of Smaug*, along with other notable guests, James Cameron, director of *Titanic* and *Avatar*, and Chinese actress Yao Chen wearing Haute Couture by Georges Hobeika and a pair of Elf-ears!

Peter Jackson is accompanied by his daughter, Katie, who, back in 2001, was one of the hobbit children in *The Fellowship of the Ring* listening to Ian Holm's Bilbo recounting his exploits with the three Trolls (now depicted in the new film). Indeed, these monstrous creatures (fortunately now safely turned to stone) are, today, looming above the red carpet.

Outside a life-size replica of Bag End, Neil Finn performs his 'Song of the Lonely Mountain', after which that famous front door opens and, to the great delight of the waiting masses, out step Peter Jackson, Martin Freeman, Richard Armitage, Andy Serkis and the full complement of Dwarves, accompanied by Mayor Celia Wade-Brown and New Zealand Prime Minister, John Key. One significant absentee is the Wizard Gandalf but, via a big screen, Ian McKellen sends his love to his colleagues, adding: 'and my favourite Dwarf – *you* know who you are!'

Then, at long last, it is time to join the rest of the guests in the Embassy. 'That was an amazing experience!' says Peter. 'My adrenaline is still running! This will be the first time seeing the film with an audience, so I am really looking forward to seeing how they respond…'

The cinema lights go down and another epic journey across Middle-earth is under way…

LUCKY FOR SOME!

'NORMALLY IN A FILM, YOU WOULDN'T START WITH THIRTEEN CHARACTERS WHO ARE ALL VERY SIMILAR.' CO-PRODUCER AND SCREENWRITER, PHILIPPA BOYENS, IS DESCRIBING ONE OF THE MAJOR CHALLENGES THAT FACED THE MAKERS OF *THE HOBBIT.* 'THERE'S JUST TOO MANY OF THEM TO ASK THE AUDIENCE TO GET TO KNOW.'

But that's the demand that J.R.R. Tolkien makes with his book and there's no getting around it. 'The book may be called *The Hobbit*,' says Philippa, 'but really central to the story in many ways is another race, that of the Dwarves. The audience, like the reader, meets them, literally, in a mad tumble: they come at you, all thirteen of them, pretty much full-on – because, essentially, they *are* full-on characters. But what I love about them and what I think works is that while they are strange and larger than life, at the same time they are entirely familiar.'

Having collaborated with Peter Jackson and Fran Walsh on the screenplays for *The Lord of the Rings* trilogy, Philippa has a clear perspective on that work and its predecessor: '*The Lord of the Rings* has incredibly passionate fans, it's one of those books that, once people have discovered it, they're devoted to it for the rest of their lives. But *The Hobbit* works in a different way: I think it's fair to say that, of all Professor Tolkien's works, it is the most beloved. Translated into numerous languages, it's been read for seventy-five years, and is still being read today.'

Taking on that reputation was, says Philippa, somewhat daunting: 'It was a little scary because *The Hobbit* is cherished by a wider range of readers than *The Lord of the Rings*. Over the years, we received a lot of letters from children who'd seen the trilogy, and were asking, "When are you going to make *The Hobbit*?" So, when we finally came to do it, we understood that there was a huge potential audience out there – not just of adults, but also kids – who really wanted to see this film. At the same time, because *The Hobbit* had to sit within the world of *Rings*, it couldn't just be a film of a children's book. Since we were able to draw not only on Tolkien's trilogy, but also the appendices to that work, we had access to a more detailed history of Middle-earth than you find in the pages of *The Hobbit*, and were able to use that to inform and give context to our storytelling.'

One of those contextualizing themes was the history of the Dwarven race and centuries-long legacy of conflict and animosity existing between the Dwarves and the Elves and other races of Middle-earth. What was essential, however, was to give each of the thirteen members of Thorin's Company their own individual characteristics. 'We always knew,' says Philippa, 'that we were going to have to pull off a trick to make that work; but having said that, we had made a film with a fellowship of nine main characters, and one of the things that I'd learned as a writer was that, if you let the actors inhabit those characters, they will help you bring them to life. So, you have to trust that process, and you also have to trust that the audience will get to know the different characters as they begin to reveal themselves and the journey advances. Having said that, we worked really hard to distinguish the Dwarves from one another and define their personalities.'

OPPOSITE: **Peter wonders whether he's a hobbit or a Dwarf.** ABOVE: **Peter, Bilbo and the Dwarves try to guess in which direction the Lonely Mountain is.** BELOW: **Bilbo and the Dwarves wonder whether they are a bit like Peter Jackson.**

Alongside those individual character developments was the way in which the entire group functioned – and, sometimes, malfunctioned! 'They might fight passionately amongst themselves,' laughs Philippa, 'but if you're an outsider and you take on one of them, you take them all on. We loved the notion that, within the group, there are tensions and arguments, but in the end the bond between them cannot be broken: they will rise together and, if necessary, fall together. That's an interesting dynamic and when you add into the mix a hobbit, who is so very unlike the Dwarves in background and temperament, that, in terms of visual storytelling, is a great gift.'

For Peter Jackson, says Philippa, the 'thirteen' were, initially, not the most welcome aspect of tackling *The Hobbit*: 'He was very aware that the number of Dwarves was going to be an issue, but, in the end, he fell in love with and enjoyed each and every one of those characters so much that he found a way to make it work and to bring that whole group together on screen, which is one of his great talents as a filmmaker.'

What's more, Philippa sees a kinship between the characters and the director: 'I know a lot of people think that Pete is a hobbit, but he also has an affinity with the Dwarves. This came out as soon as he started interacting with the group of actors playing them: they have a kind of raucous, rollicking quality and an irreverent sense of humour that is entirely Pete. So it was a natural fit and I can now see a little bit of Dwarf in Peter and a lot of Peter in all those Dwarves!'

A Hobbit's Thoughts

MARTIN FREEMAN ON BEING BILBO

'I WAS VERY AWARE OF NOT WANTING TO BE THE FIRST ANNOYING HOBBIT IN MOVIE MIDDLE-EARTH.' MARTIN FREEMAN IS TALKING ABOUT BEING BILBO. 'ABSOLUTELY NOT WANTING TO BE: "OH, I'M A HOBBIT AND I'M SWEET AND ENDEARING!" I WANTED TO GIVE THE CHARACTER THE RESPECT OF BEING GROUNDED AND THREE-DIMENSIONAL.'

At forty-one, Martin is ten years younger than Bilbo at the time of his adventure, but he is not worried by the age gap: 'Their time is different to ours because they live longer and, anyway, fifty is the new forty for hobbits! Actually, age isn't really something I think about in connection with the part, because I think – as we all do – that I am still really young. It's only when I see the numbers written down that I think, "God, that's me now!" So, essentially whatever's in my head when I see myself in the mirror is Bilbo!'

In taking on the role, Martin was unconcerned at the prospect of playing someone from an imaginary race of beings: 'I approached Bilbo's physicality simply as playing a character, rather than playing a different species. I just looked at his characteristics, listened to what he said about himself and what others said about him and all the basic acting stuff. What struck me was a certain timidity, a hesitancy, because his world is Bag End and Hobbiton, and everything beyond that is a little bit scary – certainly when a load of strange Dwarves and a Wizard turn up.'

There was also, returning to the subject of age, a youthful quality about hobbits – certainly as far as their appearance is concerned: 'You've got Harpo Marx-style hair for a start (or, at best case, Keith Richards' seventies hair) and big old feet and you're wearing shorts (well, more like lederhosen) and braces. None of that conjures up being a merciless warrior, and it doesn't conjure up sexy either – or cool! It's a look that is totally open, innocent and naïve and one that we associate with youth more than middle age. But I also know that the one thing I *mustn't* do is play Bilbo as being "childlike". At the same time, however, I'm aware that hobbits are a people who work the land and, above all else, enjoy food and drink and having a merry old time. They're not warlike, they're not cynical and they are not worldly. And, that's the interesting thing for me to play, because I feel quite worldly, I suppose – or feel

LEFT: **Bilbo is dressed and equipped ready for the next stage of his adventure to the Lonely Mountain of Erebor, but wonders what he's let himself in for once he reaches his destination** (OPPOSITE).

quite world-*weary* sometimes – and I know that's why I am sometimes cast in things, because people think I sigh well or can look convincingly cynical.'

When it comes to literary research for the role, Martin is very frank: 'I've read the book, of course, but since we started filming I don't really refer to it, because we aren't making the book, we are making these films and they contain conflations and expansions and different situations. With no disrespect to Tolkien and his source material – because the production is extremely respectful of them – I consider that I am not strictly playing Tolkien's Bilbo, but *our* Bilbo – Peter, Fran and Philippa's Bilbo.'

However, as he goes on to explain, working on the film has expanded his knowledge of the book's author: 'I've really learned a lot more about Tolkien since I've been here talking to the team – "the Holy Trinity", I call them – and, in particular, Philippa Boyens. On one occasion, I listened to her explaining about the catastrophe that befell the Dwarvish race, and she was describing it very seriously as if it were a contemporary political event in our world. I actually think Philippa probably believes Middle-earth was real!'

The film interpretation of *The Hobbit* draws on the complex antiquity that Tolkien later developed in writing *The Lord of the Rings* and whilst the novel is named after

OPPOSITE: **Bilbo starts to think the Ring he found might be very 'precious' indeed. It certainly allowed him to free himself from Gollum's clutches, and may again prove a life-saver to help the hobbit and Thorin's Company of Dwarves escape the forest of Mirkwood and the cellars of the Elven-king.** RIGHT: **Thror's map will also prove invaluable in getting Bilbo and the Dwarves to the Lonely Mountain.**

its central character, the screenplays based on the book are predominantly concerned with the impact and consequences of a history, rather than just the doings of one of the little people from the Shire. 'I think about character a lot,' says Martin, 'but I really believe that everything – including my character – is subject to the story. I'm never one of those actors who'll say, "I've got a great idea about my character! So what if it railroads the movie and takes us off course from the story? I don't care, because I want people to know this about my character, dammit!" That's simply selfish. If what you're doing isn't serving the story, then it's of no worth; it's just like sprinkles on top of a cake, it's not the actual cake. The cake is important, the decoration secondary. The thing that the Holy Trinity are in charge of is the story and it's my job – as it is for all actors – to come and serve the story because I'm never, *ever* going to be bigger than the story.'

Nevertheless, the events of that story impact heavily on Bilbo's character, as Martin acknowledges: 'He certainly undergoes a change. How to describe that? It's in what he does, how he carries himself, how he walks, speaks, and literally looks at the world. Do you look at the world sideways-on, or are you able to look at it square-on? As the story goes on, Bilbo learns to look at the world a bit more square-on. Albeit, he is still frightened, still the person he was. He's not, and is never going to be, a warrior. But on each stage of his journey, he's seeing a lot of things that he's never seen in his fifty years before. And Bilbo finds things within himself that he didn't know he had – and, more importantly, none of the others knew he had. Above all, he finds he possesses a kind of bravery. Of course, he also gets stuff wrong and is sometimes a bit of a buffoon: he's not adept with the sword, he's never been

on a horse (as you can quite clearly see from the way he holds the reins), he's not an adventurer. But he discovers hidden resources because none of us ever know how we're going to react under duress or what we're capable of until it's happening. And, you know, Bilbo reacts pretty well!'

All of which makes the hobbit the 'everyman' character with whom the moviegoer will most closely identify. 'Bilbo,' says Martin, 'is the audience's way in, because, wherever they live, they're going to have far more in common with Bilbo's life than that of any of the other characters: he goes to the market, goes to the pub, drinks, smokes, reads and is often a bit grumpy! Most people, if they had to pick one person in the story whose life is a bit like their own, it would be Bilbo. Not many people will be watching who will identify with the epic histories of the Dwarves and the Elves. And there won't be many Wizards in the audience; or Smaugs come to that – unless, of course, the bankers go to see the movie! Right, kids?'

> '*The thing that the Holy Trinity are in charge of is the story and it's my job – as it is for all actors – to come and serve the story because I'm never, ever going to be bigger than the story.*'

Bilbo & Gandalf

THE FIRST ENCOUNTER

PETER JACKSON IS DIRECTING A SCENE INTENDED AS A FLASHBACK FOR *AN UNEXPECTED JOURNEY*, IN WHICH A GATHERING OF HOBBITS, DECKED OUT IN THEIR FINEST PARTY CLOTHES, ARE ENJOYING A GRAND CELEBRATION. THE YOUNGER PARTICIPANTS – MANY OF THEM PLAYED BY CHILDREN OF THE CAST AND CREW – 'OOOOH' AND 'AAAAH' AS PETER REPEATEDLY YELLS '*BANG!*' AND HUGE LIGHTS, HIGH ABOVE THEM, FLASH IN SIMULATION OF GANDALF'S FIREWORKS THAT WILL, EVENTUALLY, BE SEEN EXPLODING OVER THE PARTY FIELD IN HOBBITON. ALTHOUGH – DUE TO AN ALREADY CROWDED STORYLINE – THIS PLEASING SEQUENCE DIDN'T MAKE IT INTO THE FINAL CUT OF THE FILM, IT CAN NOW BE ENJOYED AS PART OF THE EXTENDED EDITION DVD.

THE OFFICIAL MOVIE GUIDE

The inspiration for the scene came from the exchange between Gandalf and Bilbo Baggins when the Wizard interrupts the hobbit's early-morning smoke outside the front door of Bag End. Bilbo is determined not to have anything to do with a wandering Wizard looking for someone to send on an adventure, but what becomes clear – before Bilbo scurries back into his hobbit-hole and shuts the door – is that this is not their first meeting.

Bilbo's repeated 'Good mornings', in an attempt to be rid of the Wizard, receive an indignant response from Gandalf: 'To think,' he growls, 'that I should have lived to be "good-morning'd" by Belladonna Took's son, as if I were selling buttons at the door!'

The mention of his mother awakens in Bilbo an almost-forgotten memory of Gandalf's 'excellent fireworks' from his youth and this prompted Ian McKellen to make a suggestion to the filmmakers: 'Of course, I'm not one of the script writers,' he says, 'I'm just an actor with probably rather too much time on his hands, who offers the odd suggestion every now and again; but I thought it would be good if we could see some reason why Gandalf chooses Mr Baggins. Perhaps, I argued, it was because he remembered having met Bilbo as a feisty little lad who looked as if he might, one day, be up for an adventure; and it is this memory that leads Gandalf to come looking for him.'

As is well known to Tolkien enthusiasts, this is, indeed, how the author envisaged events and wrote about them in 'The Quest of Erebor', originally intended as part of the Appendices to *The Lord of the Rings*, but only published posthumously in *Unfinished Tales*.

Gandalf is disappointed to find that the young Bilbo he recalls has grown up into someone who, as Tolkien puts it, thinks of adventures as 'nasty, uncomfortable, disturbing things' that 'make you late for dinner'. But, being a Wizard, Gandalf doesn't give up on him, as Ian McKellen points out: 'Despite his surprise that the bright lad who had once seemed ready for anything has settled into a life of complacency, he suspects that the spirit for adventure he saw years before is still there, somewhere, inside Bilbo.'

For Philippa Boyens, Gandalf's first encounter with the young Bilbo gives an extra dimension to the story: 'It establishes an important link between the Wizard and the hobbit, as well as explaining the playful conversation between them at the door of Bag End and, for the fans, it provides an opportunity to relish another visit to Hobbiton and allow us to meet Bilbo's mother, Belladonna Took.'

Young Master Baggins is played by four-year-old Oscar

Strik, who has his own small-scale Bilbo outfit, as Costume Designer, Ann Maskrey explains: 'We wanted Bilbo's childhood clothes to prefigure what he would later become, so we created a variation of his adult travelling costume, keeping the same colours and giving him burgundy corduroy trousers and a green waistcoat with scaled-down versions of the acorn buttons that Bilbo loses when escaping from Gollum. The challenge was that it wasn't possible to use the same weight of fabric on a four-year-old as on a *forty*-year-old, because it would simply swamp him. Oscar's

THE WIZARD ON THE HOBBIT

Ian McKellen talks about Martin Freeman

One of the great joys and privileges of having made these films is to be close to Martin Freeman when he's working. Peter Jackson is often saying things like: "Keep it simple... Keep it urgent... Keep it dangerous... Keep it happy..." Those directions provide the important colours for our acting; but, within them, Martin has his own personal palette of subtlety and it's often unpredictable. He doesn't like to do the same thing twice in front of the camera, so with a multitude of takes – we might do the same scene as many as twenty times from different angles – it's very likely that Martin will give you, as the other actor, a different nuance, a different aspect of the character he's playing, so that your response, if it's going to be proper and respectful, will also change.

But his most remarkable quality as an actor, and one that I despair of emulating, is his ability to be able, with absolute clarity, to convey the fact that he's thinking, as we all often do, two different things at the same time. With Martin the inside is evident on the outside and an audience instantly knows what those thoughts are.

Martin doesn't like acting, doesn't like representing. He likes *feeling*, likes *being*. There's enormous technique at play in his work. He can do almost anything and imagine himself into almost any situation and then, with enormous delicacy, present it for the camera.

It's so difficult to analyze how Martin Freeman works, but he's better than most of us and I hope *The Hobbit* will reveal that fact to a very wide audience and establish him as a quite remarkable film actor.

ABOVE: **A portrait by Concept Artist Alan Lee of Bilbo's ancestor, The Old Took, which hangs in Bilbo's study, and (OPPOSITE) the character himself as played by Production Designer, Dan Hennah, seen here with Costume Designer, Ann Maskrey.**

waistcoat, therefore, is made from a light, summer-weight wool that was bought from a shop in London's Savile Row – known as "the golden mile of tailoring" – and happens to be most expensive wool used for any costume in the entire trilogy!'

Cast as Bilbo's mother, Belladonna, is Sonia Forbes-Adam, who, years earlier, had acted on stage with Ian McKellen. 'Her married name is Nesbitt,' says Ian McKellen, adding with a laugh, 'and she's now married to one of the Dwarves!'

For that Dwarf – Jimmy 'Bofur' Nesbitt – having his wife playing Belladonna and their two children cast as the daughters of Bard the Bowman of Lake-town, means that, as he puts it, 'We are now rather like the von Nesbitt family!'

Those Gandalf fireworks that Bilbo remembered were a regular feature at the Midsummer Eve parties organized by his grandfather, Gerontius Took – known, because he lived to be 130, as 'The Old Took'. This character provided a cameo role for someone less known for his acting talents than as the man responsible for ensuring that all the sets – including the Hobbiton Party Field – are designed, built and ready for filming: Production Designer, Dan Hennah.

A veteran of Jackson movies dating back to *The Frighteners* and including the *Rings* trilogy and *King Kong*, Dan is described by Ian McKellen as 'one of the most comfortable people to have around', adding, 'Dan always has

a ready smile, but seeing him all dressed up in his Old Took costume and smiling even more broadly than usual is really very pleasant and a reminder that, on Peter Jackson films, people who work behind the camera often get their moment in front of it and that, in a sense, *The Hobbit* is just another of Peter's home movies!'

Adjusting a capacious waistcoat, Dan recalls how he discovered that he was being considered for the cameo: 'It came as a total surprise, although I knew *something* was afoot: we were in a planning meeting and there was a lot of whispering going on and Peter was smirking. Then Producer, Carolynne Cunningham, asked if I'd like to play Bilbo's grandfather. I was really pleased, but, of course, no one told me anything about *all of this*!'

Dan is referring to his oversized hobbit ears and feet and an enormous prosthetic nose. 'They did, however, say that I'd have to shave off my beard – which, after forty years, was really rather alarming!'

Once over the initial shock, however, Dan duly applied the razor and, in preparation for his performance, grew an impressive pair of 'mutton-chop' side-whiskers and allowed his hair to develop into a mane of silver ringlets.

Dan's wife, Art Department Manager, Chris Hennah, found the transformation somewhat perplexing, never having seen him without a beard during their entire married life and being far from enthusiastic about the newly acquired whiskers.

Waiting to go on set and join the flock of hobbit boys and girls eager for the firework display to start, Dan runs a hand across his naked chin. 'As soon as we've shot this scene,' he says, 'I'm going to start growing the beard again!'

'*And*,' says Chris, who happens to be passing, 'those mutton-chops will definitely have to *go*!'

THE HOBBIT ON THE WIZARD

Martin Freeman talks about Ian McKellen

He's lovely. I instantly liked him. Ian has beautiful poise and his work as Gandalf is filled with a wonderful humanity. He's generous. He's funny. He's humble.

He has no weirdness at all about status. I mean, he's a 'Sir', but he treats that in the way that it should be treated – which is not at all seriously! He's a fellow soldier: not an officer, just rank and file. He's simply one of the cast – an *amazingly good* member of the cast, but still one of us. And that's how he sets himself up.

I've sometimes thought that if he wasn't Sir Ian McKellen, but just a regular, jobbing actor, you would still be saying, "God, but he's good!" Sometimes you work with people – senior actors who have a great reputation – and it's really nice when you can say there's a very good reason why they've got this reputation, a reason why people like them so much, and that's because they're really good – really, bloody good! And Ian is so good, that when you're watching him act you definitely want to be better and when you're working with him you actually feel yourself *getting* better.

Róisín Carty, Supervising Dialect Coach

TALKING TOLKIEN

'ACTORS NEED TO HAVE TRUST IN THEIR COACH; THEY NEED TO KNOW THAT YOU'RE NEITHER A PERFORMER NOR A DIRECTOR BUT ARE JUST THERE TO HELP THEM REACH THE RIGHT SOUNDS FOR WHAT THEIR CHARACTERS HAVE TO SAY.' RÓISÍN CARTY, SUPERVISING DIALECT COACH ON *THE HOBBIT*, IS RETURNING TO THE WORLD OF MIDDLE-EARTH, HAVING PREVIOUSLY SERVED AS ASSISTANT COACH ON *THE LORD OF THE RINGS*. UNLIKE MOST OTHER MEMBERS OF THE CREW, HER CONTRIBUTION TO THE FILMS, THOUGH VITAL, REMAINS COMPLETELY UNSEEN. WHILST THE SCREENWRITERS ARE CONCERNED WITH WHAT THE CHARACTERS SAY, RÓISÍN AND HER TEAM FOCUS ON *HOW THEY SAY IT*.

Having studied for a degree in speech sciences at University College London with a view to being a speech therapist, Róisín became increasingly interested in drama and, after gaining her degree, went to the Central School of Speech and Drama to take a post-graduate diploma course in voice teaching. In their different ways, both periods of study were equipping Róisín for her later work with the Dwarves and Elves and other races created by J.R.R. Tolkien: 'I developed a love of linguistics, and the way in which people communicate, through language and became increasingly fascinated by accents and how they linked up with my knowledge of phonetics.'

After acting as voice coach on the film *Waking Ned*, Róisín learned of a prospective project to film *The Lord of the Rings* and, knowing the importance of languages in Tolkien's writings, she offered her services. Shortly afterwards, she found herself in New Zealand getting to grips with the varying nuances of Tolkien's Elvish languages of Quenya and Sindarin that are now being taught to a new generation of Elves.

'Quenya,' says Róisín, 'is the language of the High Elves and tends to be used poetically or ritualistically for spells, incantations and quotations from ancient sources. And,

rather like such well-known prayers as the "Our Father" or the "Hail Mary", there is a way of speaking them that has been established across centuries so that it is spoken or recited almost without thinking of the individual words so much as the overall feeling which they convey.'

In contrast, it was agreed that Sindarin should sound like a living language that was naturally spoken by the Elves and, occasionally, by other bilingual characters such as Gandalf and his fellow Wizards. 'What is essential,' says Róisín, 'is that it shouldn't sound like someone reciting Latin or reading something they had *learned* to say in a particular way, but a language that the characters have grown up speaking. It has to be beautiful and lyrical, but the speech patterns shouldn't ever sound contrived, and it is vitally important to allow the actor to have a clear understanding of the words they are saying, so as to be able to put their own intonation pattern onto the phrases.'

The linguistic challenges faced on *The Hobbit* are not confined to the Elves, but affect all the other races featured in the film, in particular the Dwarves. One of the ways in which the filmmakers tackled the challenge of having thirteen central characters was to group them into family units. This concept fitted with the notion of a diaspora in which the Dwarves, driven out of their homelands, had dispersed to various parts of Middle-earth where they developed different accents.

The starting point for deciding those accents was always rooted in the native vocal characteristics of one or more of the actors in each group: 'Part of our approach,' says Róisín, 'is always to listen to the accent of actors and see if there's a way in which that can enrich what they bring to their roles. On *The Hobbit*, Peter, Fran and Philippa wanted certain actors to be the model for the accent of their particular Dwarf family. So, in the case of Ken Stott and Graham McTavish, playing brothers Balin and Dwalin, the natural Scottish accents of both actors determined how the characters would speak and helped establish their kinship.'

With several of the groups, the chosen accent was that of one particular actor and had to be adopted by the actors playing the other family members, as Róisín explains: 'It was decided that Richard Armitage as Thorin should keep something of his own Leicestershire accent because it gave him stature and gravitas and allowed him to sound regal while, at the same time, having an earthiness that rooted him in the history of his people. That decision made, Dean O'Gorman and Aidan Turner as Thorin's nephews, Fili and Kili, took their vocal lead from their uncle's accent.'

James Nesbitt was born in Ballymena, County Antrim, in Northern Ireland and his portrayal of Bofur draws on memories of family voices heard when he was growing up. 'The Northern Irish accent,' says Róisín, 'can sometimes sound harsh, but Jimmy uses a softer, country accent that gives the character warmth and sincerity and enhances the loyalty and compassion that, almost alone among the Dwarves, Bofur shows towards Bilbo.'

Although, at the beginning of *The Hobbit*, neither Bofur's brother, Bombur, nor his cousin, Bifur, have many – or *any* – lines, actors Stephen Hunter and William Kircher committed themselves to mastering the accent used by James, as Róisín reveals: 'When we were preparing to begin filming, Stephen and William attended accent sessions with Jimmy because Stephen wanted to be primed in case, at some later point in the films, he had to speak in character. William – who, as Bifur, has only occasional brief speeches in Ancient Dwarvish (or Khuzdul, which no one else understands) – wanted to have a feel for the accent so that his rare vocal moments or even his occasional grunts and mumbles could be delivered with a Northern Irish intonation.'

The accent model for Gloin and Oin was that of an actor not in *The Hobbit* but in *The Lord of the Rings*. John Rhys-Davies' distinctive Welsh-derived accent for Gimli was adopted by New Zealanders John Callen and Peter Hambleton in portraying characters who are Gimli's father and uncle.

OPPOSITE: **Supervising Dialect Coach, Róisín Carty, pictured with Elijah Wood as Frodo as he prepares to film his scenes with Ian Holm at London's Pinewood Studios.** ABOVE: **Because Peter filmed the Elves at an even higher frame rate than normal, Galadriel's speech comes through at a slightly slower tempo, creating a dream-like, magical quality.**

ABOVE: Elvish as spoken in the films would have its roots in Welsh and Finnish, just as Tolkien had envisaged, and when English is spoken at the White Council, particularly by the Elves, care was taken to enunciate each letter. OPPOSITE: Much time was spent by the Dialect Coaches in working with each member of Thorin's Company to create distinctive regional accents for the Dwarves in order to convey how widespread the race had become.

The fact that Dori, Ori and Nori, according to their character back-stories, share a mother but have three different fathers, allowed the trio to have a diversity of accents within their family group, as Róisín explains: 'Mark Hadlow has a lovely comic Lancashire accent for Dori, the 'mother' character who is always fretting, nagging and nit-picking; Ori has a trace of Adam Brown's native West Berkshire accent with its subtle hint of country that seems particularly suited to the character's youth and innocence; and Nori has a more urban accent that fits with his wide-boy, cheeky-chappie, dodgy-dealer persona.'

One of the challenges facing Róisín and her colleagues is the diversity of natural accents found amongst a cast featuring actors from various parts of the British Isles and assorted American States as well as from Australia and New Zealand: 'The films aim to transport moviegoers to another world and it is vitally important that audiences are not pulled out of that world by being confused by characters' speech or distracted by accent-spotting. Essentially we wanted the film to capture that unique quality of Tolkien's writings: a strong sense of being in a realm that is very different to our own yet possesses similarities that we recognize. So, as a department, we came up with the phrase "Accents of Other-where", to remind us that what we are all trying to create is a mood that is more to do with "time" than "place": accents need to be familiar but not immediately located in a particular country or region and, most importantly, not too modern, not too much of our time.'

So how does the dialect coach tackle the task of instructing – sometimes correcting – actors who already have a lot of things on their mind, such as coping with make-up, costumes and props, where to stand, when to

'The films aim to transport moviegoers to another world and it is vitally important that audiences are not pulled out of that world by being confused by characters' speech or distracted by accent-spotting.'

THE OFFICIAL MOVIE GUIDE

LEITH McPHERSON:
UNLOCKING THE VOICE WITHIN

'You have to try and pick the lock of the actor's mind.'

Dialect Coach, Leith McPherson, is describing how she helps actors cope with the challenge of correctly pronouncing words and names in the various languages of Middle-earth. 'The secret is finding the right tools to make something stick; but making it sticky will be different for every single actor, and it will be different on every single day.'

There are, it seems, certain times when actors find it harder to remember their lines than at others. 'First thing after lunch is a common danger zone,' says Leith. 'They quite often come back from eating and find that their lines have gone, totally wiped! It's as if the brain has switched off the memory functions in order to be able to digest lunch properly!'

Ways of instilling pronunciations into actors' memories are many and various: 'Some actors find it helpful to be given a physical movement to aid them in remembering the stressing required for the correct pronunciation of a word. So if you can link, say, throwing a ball whilst saying Gandalf's Elvish name, "Mithrandir", and practice that several times, when you stop doing the movement you'll find that the physical impulse remains and connects to the sound of the word that needs to be remembered.'

There are some actors who need to understand what is happening anatomically when they speak. 'For them,' Leith says, 'I draw a cross-section of the mouth, indicating the shape needed to make a particular vowel-sound. On other occasions, we will take a word that an actor finds particularly difficult and change it into a new word by spelling it in the way in which it should be said. These are just a few of the techniques that can allow you to pick an actor's mind, get past the defences in the brain, and work with them so they can cope with that incredibly demanding and pressurized moment of delivering difficult lines.'

move and the basic need to remember their lines? 'You need a lot of experience,' says Róisín, 'and, more than anything, a lot of natural diplomacy! The people you are helping need to feel at ease with you. I personally think it's helpful that they know that I simply love language, words and the differences in sounds and that I've no desire to be in front of a camera or in the limelight.'

The logistics of advising during filming also require an ability to judge not just what advice to give, but how and when to give it: 'If an actor is speaking on set and you hear something that is not quite right, you know that you have to correct the error as soon as possible because it's not going to be useful if the same mistake is made take after take.'

The secret, however, is timing: 'If there's a break between takes – maybe to check hair and make-up – you have to get in there and be as fast, small and invisible as possible! Without getting in the way of the hair and make-up folk, because their work is as equally important, you can often manage to whisper in the actor's ear or – where you've established a relationship with the actor and have possibly agreed a visual shorthand – give them a quick non-verbal clue. Part of our role is being supportive, knowing when an actor needs you there to give them a reassuring wink or a thumbs-up, but also knowing when an actor *doesn't* want to see you, because if they do, they'll start thinking about the language or the accent, rather than the acting. Each actor needs something special from us and it's our job to know what that is and be there to give it.'

Joe Letteri, Senior Visual Effects Supervisor

THE WIZARD OF WETA

'**A**UDIENCES WANT TO SEE SOMETHING THAT IS LARGER THAN LIFE AND WE'RE HELPING THESE BIG FANTASY FILMS BE MADE TO ACHIEVE JUST THAT.' MULTI-OSCAR-AND-BAFTA-AWARD-WINNING SENIOR VISUAL EFFECTS SUPERVISOR AT WETA DIGITAL, JOE LETTERI, IS TALKING ABOUT HIS ORGANIZATION'S WORK ON THE *HOBBIT* TRILOGY. 'OUR WORK IS THERE, THROUGHOUT THE FILMS, EVEN IF YOU'RE NOT AWARE OF IT: THOUSANDS OF SHOTS ACROSS THREE FILMS FROM COMPLETELY DIGITAL ENVIRONMENTS TO PAINTING OUT A STRAY CAR IN THE BACKGROUND.'

For the past twenty-four years, Joe has worked on some iconic special effects movies such as *Jurassic Park*, *Mission: Impossible* and *Star Wars: Episode IV – A New Hope*. Since joining Weta Digital for *The Lord of The Rings: The Two Towers*, he has supervised the effects not only on Peter Jackson's films, *The Lord of the Rings: The Return of the King*, *King Kong*, *The Lovely Bones* and *The Adventures of* *Tintin: The Secret of the Unicorn* but also *Van Helsing*, *I, Robot*, *X-Men: The Last Stand*, *Avatar* and *Rise of the Planet of the Apes*.

Revisiting Middle-earth for *The Hobbit* was a challenge to be savoured. 'It was an exciting prospect,' says Joe, 'being able to bring a fresh perspective as well as greater detail and richness to the depiction of Tolkien's world on

OPPOSITE: **A climactic moment from the first film dramatically showcases the contribution of Weta Digital to the production.** ABOVE: **Advances in both digital and motion capture technology ensured that the Eagles would look as real as the New Zealand landscape they flew over, and that Gollum would look as real as his human co-stars.**

screen, especially knowing that the films would be viewed in 3D and 48 frames per second.'

The films required the visualization of a range of beings and creatures, from hedgehogs and outsized rabbits to armies of Goblins, Stone Giants and a huge, fire-breathing Dragon. There was also an opportunity to be reacquainted with some of the denizens of Middle-earth previously encountered in the *Rings* trilogy.

'There's a tradition that every time we see the creatures in each film they are slightly different from the last time we met them. For example, if you look at the Trolls from *The Fellowship of the Ring* through to *The Return of the King*, you see three distinct variations: each time we tackled them, we treated them as if they were a different tribe and the Trolls in *The Hobbit* now represent a fourth variety.'

That said, when the Trolls are finally turned into stone, we see them in the familiar pose first glimpsed in *Fellowship*, back in 2001, when Frodo, Sam, Merry and Pippin made camp in the shadow of their fossilized remains.

Similar developments occurred with two other denizens of Middle-earth, as Joe explains: 'This time the Wargs are truer to the Northern European wolf-look, but we've sharpened up their features and made them considerably more sinister. As for the Eagles, they feature more prominently than in the *Rings* films – and in increased numbers – but it's very hard to make them look more majestic than the real birds; so, instead, we worked on their flight movement and on perfecting the intricate detailing of their feathers.'

The key returning character, of course, was Gollum. 'In the ensuing years we've achieved new levels of animated sophistication with *King Kong*, *Avatar* and *Rise* *of the Planet of the Apes*, so to be able to go back and revisit Gollum with all that experience under our belts was always going to be a highlight for us. We were able to look at all those things we had almost got right with the newly acquired knowledge of how to make corrections and improvements. The result? Gollum looks like he did – we *know* him – but we have been able to add more nuances to his performance, such as the detailing in the eyes, how the muscles move under the skin and the way in which his hair moves – things we did not know how to do a decade ago. For a time we experimented with making him look a little younger, giving him more hair, putting back some of his teeth, but since, within his life-span, the passage of sixty years is negligible, we eventually decided to leave him more or less the same other than to take away the scars that resulted from his later torture in Sauron's dungeons in Mordor.'

The process of upgrading Gollum was greatly assisted by a better use of motion-capture. 'On *The Two Towers*,' recalls Joe, 'MoCap was experimental, on *King Kong* we found we could capture face as well as body, on *Avatar* we discovered how to put the two together in a virtual world, and for *Rise of the Planet of the Apes* we figured out how to do it live on a set. By the time we got to *The Hobbit* we were able to do it all with the shots between Gollum and Bilbo. They were the first scenes of the entire trilogy that we shot: Andy Serkis and Martin Freeman together in their characters and MoCap cameras hidden all around the set. We recorded Andy's performance and that was what went straight into the film. Using technology that we have been developing for ten years, we had finally come full circle. Filming 'Riddles in the Dark' was quite a homecoming.'

Replacing the physical with digitized substitutes extends to the cast members themselves, all of whom now have a digital double ready and able to take over in tricky scenes.

A vital part of Weta Digital's work on *The Hobbit* is in helping create the exotic and fantastical sets. Whereas, on *The Lord of the Rings*, locations such as Rivendell, Orthanc and Minas Tirith were realized using large, exquisitely sculpted miniature models, on *The Hobbit* the demands of 3D and 48 frames per second would have meant that any miniatures would have needed to be massive to provide the necessary detail, and as such would have required a huge sound stage on which to film them.

It was, therefore, more practical to create a digital set, as Joe explains: 'Everything that happens in the immediate area around the actors you can shoot as normal film: you want enough actual set so that everyone has a sense of the mood and the environment framing the action – doors, passageways, any objects the actors have to handle or work with – but anything that fills out the scene around it can be visualized digitally.'

Replacing the physical with digitized substitutes extends to the cast members themselves, all of whom now have a digital double ready and able to take over in tricky

scenes. 'It has always been the case,' says Joe, 'that an actor in a film will be played at some point or other by someone else, such as a stunt double for sequences that are too dangerous or, in our films, a scale double to solve problems arising from the size difference between the different races of Middle-earth. Digital doubles are just an extension of that: just as we create digital environments because it is sometimes impossible to actually build the huge sets called for in the script, there are times when characters are required to be involved in actions that are too dangerous or just downright impossible, and that's where we can use an actor's digital double.'

ABOVE: **A stunt performer in a motion-capture suit would be replaced by a fully digital Goblin, whose features could be stretched to something less than human.** RIGHT: **Bilbo and the Rivendell studio set would be enhanced with a fully digital valley complete with animated waterfalls.** OVERLEAF: **Even with the stunning vistas that New Zealand has to offer, realizing the full spectacle of the city of Dale and its mountainside location would have been impossible without digital technology.**

Just such a scene was the passage over the Misty Mountains where the Dwarves encounter the rock-hurling Stone Giants. 'You can't put performers in that kind of danger,' says Joe, 'in order to get even a reasonable portrayal of what is supposed to be happening, so we did it digitally.'

Another example where digital doubling would be called for is the sequence in the Goblin caverns: 'Having costumed actors on set is great for the director to envision the scene and for the actors to work with, but if you've an actor running around in a Goblin costume, any wrinkling or folding of the prosthetics that doesn't move like skin is going to look totally unrealistic. So as you are digitally replacing elements that don't work, you might just as well replace those actors with fully digital characters for the final picture.'

On *An Unexpected Journey*, Weta Digital provided in the region of 2,200 digital shots. With such a workload, the decision to extend *The Hobbit* from two films to three proved something of a relief, as Joe remembers with a laugh: 'There was so much still facing us – all sorts of places and creatures – that could now get moved into the second film! But that sense of relief was all too brief, because shortly afterwards we found out that the film was going to open with a prologue which required more than enough work to take the place of what we'd just been saved from doing!'

So how do Weta achieve the demands made on them and meet the seemingly impossible deadlines? 'You have to keep asking yourself: "If I were sitting in the audience watching a scene, would I feel that I am *in* the world for every single frame of film?" Nothing must ever take you out of the story. That has to be our focus and motivation: whatever is needed to make that work, we'll figure out. Sometimes that means that we don't sleep as much as we'd like and a lot of people worked very hard for long hours over many months, but you have just the one chance to get it right; you only have until the deadline to get those images on the screen. Once that deadline has passed, *then* you can sleep!'

THE DWARVES' QUEST OF EREBOR

'IT'S ESSENTIALLY ABOUT US GOING TO KNOCK OUT SMAUG THE DRAGON AND TAKE BACK THE MOUNTAIN – RECOVERING DWARF-LAND AND ALL THE GOLD AS WELL.' THAT'S BOMBUR'S VIEW OF THE QUEST OF EREBOR, AS EXPRESSED BY ACTOR, STEPHEN HUNTER. 'I GUESS IT MEANS DIFFERENT THINGS FOR DIFFERENT PEOPLE, BECAUSE FOR THE GUYS WHO ARE ROYALTY IT'S THEIR GOLD AND THEY'RE QUITE FOCUSED ON THE TREASURE. WHEREAS FROM BOFUR'S, BIFUR'S AND MY POINT OF VIEW, IT MEANS WE'LL HOPEFULLY GET PAID HANDSOMELY, WHICH WILL PROVIDE FOOD AND EVERYTHING ELSE WE NEED FOR OUR FAMILY.'

Richard Armitage, playing Thorin, provides the 'royal' perspective: 'The Quest of Erebor is the chance for the Dwarves to reclaim their inheritance. Thorin's father, Thrain, longed to reclaim their homeland but he was taken by Orcs before he could attempt the quest, which is why Thorin now assumes that burden. Interestingly, the name "Thrain" translates as "yearner" and "Thorin" as "darer" and, in a way, Thrain is the one who yearned to recover the lost kingdom and its gold, but couldn't achieve it, while Thorin is the one who dares to do it.'

However, as Jed Brophy, who plays Nori, points out the Quest is not simply about the treasure that Smaug has purloined for his Dragon-hoard: 'Gold may, ostensibly, seem to be the primary reason, but from the back-story written by Tolkien it is clear that throughout their history they were considered a lesser race than the Elves, so knowing the way that their minds work, this Quest for regaining Erebor is, as much as anything, about recovering their self-respect, not just as individuals but as a race.'

Aidan Turner, who plays Kili, agrees: 'They've been brought up with so many ancient songs and stories of battles, victories and defeats and it is now their destiny to travel to the Lonely Mountain and attempt to reclaim their lost treasure, and possibly their lost homeland. Apart from the fact that Dwarves are semi-obsessed with material goods, it is something that they just need to do, as a matter of pride and for the survival of their people.'

LEFT: **Unfortunately, the Dwarves Dori, (Mark Hadlow), Oin (John Callen), Gloin (Peter Hambleton) and Bifur (William Kircher) find that eating at Lake-town has less to offer than Bag End did. OPPOSITE: A king returns to claim his kingdom.**

RIGHT: **Bilbo and the Dwarves, now somewhat bedraggled after their experience as the Elven-king's guests, receive an uncertain welcome at Lake-town.** OPPOSITE: **Bifur (William Kircher), Ori (Adam Brown) and Nori (Jed Brophy) outside the Lonely Mountain's secret door; Bofur (James Nesbitt) wonders if leaving Bard's house is a good idea.**

As Oin's John Callen puts it: 'The Quest is as much about dignity and re-establishing their rights of ownership as it is about regaining whatever coinage might be involved. Being miners, the Dwarves unearthed things of great value and that was the resource from which they built their great kingdom. But all that prosperity has been taken from them by the Dragon, who is a terrorist, taking what he wants in the way terrorists do: with force and firepower. Robbed and demeaned by this great beast who is lying there, inside their Mountain, right on top of their heaped-up wealth, motivates them to avenge their suffering and regain that lost heritage.'

'It is a very personal fight,' says William Kircher, in character as Bifur. 'About two hundred years ago, Smaug killed thousands of our ancestors and took our kingdom. As a result, we were dispossessed and went off in different directions into exile, since then we have been trying to survive, eking out a living as best we can. Now, the Dwarvish race is gradually diminishing so our desire to take back Erebor is about reclaiming our racial identity and what we feel is spiritually ours by right. That's why we're up for the fight.'

'Even though Balin is a little reluctant to be part of this adventure,' notes Ken Stott, 'he recognizes that the injuries and offences suffered by the Dwarves still rankle and that, as a group, everybody is on board to see the Quest through to the end.'

For James Nesbitt, playing Bofur, the Quest is basically a matter of right and wrong: 'The Dwarves have been wronged and it is time to put right that wrong. There's something very pure and simple about what they are trying to do: righting a wrong. The British playwright, Terence Rattigan has a character in his play, *The Winslow Boy*, that says "Right has been done," and when someone asks if he is talking about justice he replies: "No, not justice. Right. Easy to do justice. Very hard to do right." That's what the Dwarves are trying to do – what is essentially right.'

As the story of the Quest unfolds on screen in *The Hobbit* trilogy, the Company of Dwarves have reason to hope that their old enemy the Dragon may no longer pose a threat. 'Oin is a prognosticator,' says the actor who plays him, John Callen. 'He can read signs and portents and from them foresee the future, as he explains during the meeting in Bag End: "Ravens have been seen flying back to the Mountain, as it was foretold: When the birds of old return to Erebor, the reign of the beast will end." Oin argues that if Smaug is dead, the reign of terror over and all those stolen goodies just lying there under the Mountain, unprotected, it's time to get back there and pick them up!'

'If Smaug is dead,' says Richard Armitage, 'then many will come to claim or to take. There's a sense that something's happening at the Mountain and if the Dwarves don't act now, others will get there first. So there's an itch, a need, a desire to do just that – particularly with Thorin. It is a hundred years to the day since his father, Thráin, set

> *'It's time to go and retrieve their birthright: their wealth and their homeland. Is it a long shot? No, because there's gold at the end of the journey, waiting for them, right there under that Mountain.'*

out for Erebor and disappeared; the portents indicate that they have cause to hope and Thorin feels that if he doesn't do it now, he never will. But then, when they get to Bag End and Gandalf pulls out the map and the key to the secret door, it's no longer a certainty that the Dragon is dead, it's now nothing more than speculation…'

So, as Peter Hambleton, who plays Gloin, points out: 'Yes, the odds are ridiculous and, yes, they're an eccentric bunch of characters, but, of course, that's what makes following their journey so much fun.'

But Adam Brown, playing the youngest of the Dwarves, Ori, doesn't think the odds are quite as bad as some others believe: 'It's time to go and retrieve their birthright: their wealth and their homeland. Is it a long shot? No, because there's gold at the end of the journey, waiting for them, right there under that Mountain.'

Considering what the Dwarves may be facing on their arrival at the Lonely Mountain, how well are they equipped? 'They need to be brave, resourceful and inventive,' says New Zealander, Peter Hambleton, 'and, fortunately, they are all of those things. There's an almost Kiwi-like "can-do" attitude to the group. They're not a great army, they're more in the nature of a guerrilla force: they can move quickly, travel light and when they're in a fix, they can fight their way out of it.'

Agreeing, Dean O'Gorman, who plays Fili, adds: 'Dwarves are very passionate and very upfront with their emotions: hugging and laughing one minute, arguing and fighting the next.' Which may go some way to explain Mark 'Dori' Hadlow's view of the group:

'There's some doubt there and mistrust at the outset, but the way events unfold that has to change because they are soon fighting for their lives. All of these things make *The Hobbit* a timeless story that is totally relevant for a contemporary audience: there's fear, courage, suspicion, betrayal, danger, double-crossings and death – and humour. All the wonderful ingredients that come into any film or story these days are here in abundance!'

OPPOSITE: **This gigantic head, sculpted in polystyrene, is just the top of an enormous statue of Thorin's grandfather, Thrór, which is seen in full as the Company reach Erebor. But as they get closer it reveals a surprising secret.** ABOVE LEFT: **Dwalin (Graham McTavish) has got himself a bigger weapon to face the Dragon.** ABOVE RIGHT: **For Thorin this Quest means everything.** OVERLEAF: **Balin and his fellow Companions stand at the very threshold of their goal.**

Mikael Persbrandt

BEORN

'BEORN IS NOT WHAT HE SEEMS,' SAYS SWEDISH ACTOR, MIKAEL PERSBRANDT, 'HE'S NOT LIKE YOU AND ME. HE'S SOMETHING ELSE. THERE IS SOMETHING VERY DARK AND SAD ABOUT HIM AND YOU DON'T KNOW IF HE IS YOUR FRIEND OR ENEMY. BEORN IS A SKIN-CHANGER AND CAN SHAPE-SHIFT INTO A FEARSOME BEAR, SO BE CAREFUL.'

The concept of beings that can magically change their shape from human into animal form is one that is repeatedly found in world literature from ancient myths, legends and fairytales through to contemporary fiction.

'Beorn,' says Mikael, 'is huge and strong and even as a human there's something wild about him that you can't really understand.' So, in an attempt to get a better grasp of animal nature, the actor visited Sweden's Kolmården Wildlife Park and spent time in the wolf enclosure doing some close-range research. 'The leader of the pack came to me and was "talking" to me,' says Mikael, recalling the sense of communing he gained from the experience. 'He certainly put some energy into my ego.'

Mikael is no stranger to playing challenging and dramatic roles and is well known in his native Sweden for compelling stage, film and television performances. Winner of the 2005 Ingmar Bergman Award, Mikael has performed in plays by Shakespeare, Strindberg, Chekhov, Ibsen, Samuel Beckett and Arthur Miller. He has appeared in numerous TV dramas, notably as Gunvald Larsson in the long-running crime series, *Beck*. His extensive film career includes *In A Better World*, which won both the 2011 Golden Globe Award and the Oscar for Best Foreign Language Film.

As someone who had been a childhood fan of Tolkien, Mikael was thrilled to get a role in *The Hobbit*. 'I read all the books when I was twelve or thirteen years old,' he says, 'in that period when fantasy erupts in you! The structure of

saga and the heroism is very appealing to a young person. At that age, it is quite easy to see the difference between the light stuff and dark stuff. I think it's a way to understand the world and is also a bit of escape. I was totally in that realm for a couple of years, so it's a fantastic adventure to be in the movies.'

Although an exponent of the 'method' school of acting, Mikael has not pursued this approach in playing Beorn: 'My only advice to myself was, number one, listen to Peter and his vision and try to follow that, and then, for the rest of it, "less is more".'

One element of the job that turned out to be more rather than less was the two-and-a-half-hours spent each day in the make-up chair. 'Still,' he reflects philosophically, 'I got away with less than some of the Dwarves. There *is* a nose job and a set of teeth. However,' he adds with a laugh, 'that's something that happens to many people in Hollywood – they shape-shift a lot there! Luckily, I can take it off when the day is done.'

The nose, chosen from half a dozen prototypes, could be a boxer's and the teeth are sharper and more animal-like. 'They don't make my English any better,' admits Mikael, 'but I'm struggling with it. Happily the ears and eyes are my own!'

Beorn also has long hair that continues down his back like a horse's mane. Mikael's description of Beorn's appearance is interesting: 'He is bit like a mixture between a hard

THE OFFICIAL MOVIE GUIDE

Reflecting on the actor's lot, Mikael says, 'It's an odd job. The first day on a movie with a new character is always strange and, in a way, scary because, whatever characteristics you establish when you shoot your first scene – even if it is in the middle of the movie – you have to live with that character later on.'

When he eventually got to film the scene with Gandalf and the Dwarves, Mikael was impressed with the set for Beorn's house with its livestock – big horses and huge long-horned cows – and a giant-sized axe with which Beorn is seen chopping wood. 'It was huge with a big blade,' he says, 'really heavy – probably twenty kilos – and you have to get it right. It was kind of problematic, but interesting, and it feels good when you make it work.'

Being a sequence involving three scales of characters, there were several variously sized axes, depending on who was seen in relation to it. Regardless of the size of the axe (Beorn-scale, Dwarf-scale and an in-between Gandalf-scale), one thing is certain – Mikael chopped a *lot* of wood: 'With small axes and big axes, I chopped about a thousand trees! It wasn't a problem because, for many years, I've been living in a house by the sea outside Stockholm and chopping my own wood; and it's fun to have something *real* to do when starting a scene.'

The interior of Beorn's house was especially striking with its huge table and chairs built to a gigantic scale that would be appropriate for the height of the diminutive Dwarves. There was only one drawback: 'Beorn is so big, when it came to my turn to face the camera; I had to go into another, small, green-screen studio with thirteen tennis

rocker from the nineteen-seventies and a horse at full speed on some Argentinian savannah.'

Referring to his costume, Mikael says, 'Beorn is one hundred per cent pure vegan guy, so everything he wears is made from wool.' Indeed, since he has the ability to skin-change into an animal, there is no leather, fur or anything that would have involved killing an animal. Even his boots are made out of wool. 'Yes,' says Mikael, 'it's a good dress-code for a skin-changer.'

In Old Norse literature, there are accounts of warriors who, on the eve of a battle, would work themselves up into a frenzy of anger until they were in a state of altered consciousness and virtually out of control. Since they often fought wearing the hide of a bear, they became known as 'berserkers', a name that probably originated from the merging of the Norse words for 'bear' and 'shirt'.

As Andrew Baker, Creature and Character Designer at Weta Digital, explains, this was one of the many inspirations behind Beorn's character when he shape-shifts into animal form: 'We wanted to try and capture something of the ferocity of the berserker when Beorn's in his bear mode; a force of nature going absolutely crazy and taking out anything that stands in his way.'

balls on sticks representing the Dwarves and a football for Gandalf! It was one of the most magnificent sets I've ever seen – representing the friendly, gentle atmosphere of my house – and I never worked in it! Sad story, huh?'

Mikael has now acted opposite his tennis-ball co-stars on numerous occasions, having made the journey from Sweden to New Zealand seven times. 'It takes approximately thirty-two hours, so you do a lot of thinking while you're on that plane. You try to read, see one or two movies and then there are still some hours left. But arriving and meeting the tennis balls again, I can always see the reason for it!'

In addition to playing Beorn in human form, Mikael has filmed motion-capture footage for the character's ursine alter ego and experimented with vocalizing his animal instincts! To help achieve this, the actor listened to recordings of bears. 'There were some thousand or more bear sounds,' he recalls, 'beautiful sounds; not just growling, but how bears talk to each other. There were angry bears, tired bears, sorry bears – even a horny bear! I practiced making a lot of bear calls and wondered at the time if I was being caught on some kind of hidden-camera show, but it was for real! I have seven litres of lungs, but Beorn's voice will be coming from fourteen-litre lungs, so I think there is going to be some shape-shifting in my voice as well.'

Returning to his experiences with the wolf-pack leader during his zoo visit, Mikael says: 'I was not afraid because I have this belief in myself and thought that if I were in serious danger I would be able to break his neck.' As it happened, his visit passed off without incident, but just one week later the same wolves attacked and killed one of their keepers. That unpredictability of wild creatures is something that Mikael has tried to bring to his characterization: 'Something is always clicking in their heads, you only have to stumble and they'll react and you're dead – *super*-dead! Same thing with Beorn: don't stumble around him!'

Top: **Peter Jackson gazes admiringly at the quality of Mikael Persbrandt's wood-chopping.** Right: **The actor and director discuss a scene inside Beorn's house; on the shelf behind can be seen beeswax candles and carved wooden animals.** Overleaf: **Beorn warns Gandalf about the journey ahead.**

BEORN'S CHESS SET

What does Beorn do on those long, dark winter nights when he is not prowling Middle-earth in the shape of a bear? That was a question that Concept Artist Alan Lee was pondering as designs for *The Hobbit* got underway. His thoughts turned to the ancient game of chess that, with variations, has been played for at least 15,000 years and that has frequently been compared to the struggles of human life. 'The chess-board is the world,' said the nineteenth century anatomist, Thomas Huxley, 'the pieces are the phenomena of the universe, the rules of the game are what we call the laws of Nature. The player on the other side is hidden from us.' All of which makes chess an appropriate pastime for Wilderland's skin-changer.

Alan Lee recalls: 'We were thinking about ways in which his dwelling and the objects in it may reflect his personality and history. The one thing that Tolkien made clear, and that we knew would be reflected in the script, was that he was a guardian of the natural world, and a fierce protector of the animals that surrounded him. We also thought that he may occupy himself with wood-carving and that his home could be richly decorated with sculpture in which human and natural forms would intertwine. I did some designs that suggested knowledge of evolution, thinking that he may be something of a natural philosopher.'

In Tolkien's book, Beorn and his guests are served dinner by animals – dogs, ponies and sheep – clearly a challenging concept for the filmmaker. 'We realized,' says Alan, 'that the animal food-servers might not make it into the film, but we wanted this part of his character to be seen in the sets and the objects around him. As well as large, totemic sculptures and pillars, we wanted to have something relatively small and detailed that, when seen in close proximity to the actors, would help with the scale. A hand-whittled chess set seemed the perfect way of demonstrating his skills and his love for animals, and gives a clue to his intelligence and to the amount of time he may have on his hands.'

So the chess pieces in Alan's designs assumed animal likenesses: 'The Kings became bears and queens were eagles; they were attended by squirrel knights and weasel bishops and with snakes for rooks or castles and hedgehogs for pawns. The sets were beautifully carved by Anneke Bester and Noel Simmonds of the Props Making department and were made in two sizes: a Beorn-scale set and a larger one to be seen in relation to the Dwarves. The same figures feature on both sides of the game, with the black or red pieces being made from darker wood while the chessboard was inlaid in a big, rough-hewn table. It was great seeing the quality of the workmanship and knowing that it would also be clearly seen by the audience!'

A game of opposing players, chess might, at first sight, seem an unlikely entertainment for a solitary character such as Beorn. Not so, says Alan: 'I've been a keen chess player and know that the lack of an opponent doesn't make you lose interest in trying to master the game!'

Bilbo must have been particularly captivated by Beorn's chess set because when, in the opening moments of *An Unexpected Journey*, the elderly hobbit goes to his chest of personal treasures in search of his journal, the sharp-eyed will notice, among the cluttered contents, one of the chess-pieces – a bear-shaped King. 'I do hope it was a *gift*,' comments Alan Lee, 'rather than a demonstration of Bilbo's talent for burglary!'

BEORN'S HOUSE

'IS BEORN FRIENDLY, OR IS HE GOING TO TURN INTO A BEAR AND EAT THEM ALL?' ASKS CONCEPT ARTIST, JOHN HOWE. MEETING THE GIANT SKIN-CHANGER IS JUST ONE OF THE MANY POSSIBLY PERILOUS ENCOUNTERS EXPERIENCED BY BILBO AND THE COMPANY OF DWARVES WHEN THEY ENTER THAT REGION OF MIDDLE-EARTH THAT TOLKIEN NAMED WILDERLAND ON HIS MAP TO *THE HOBBIT*. 'AS THE NAME SUGGESTS,' SAYS JOHN, 'WILDERLAND IS A WILD PLACE, WHERE NATURE RULES AND WHERE THE DIVISIONS BETWEEN GOOD AND EVIL, FRIENDLY AND HOSTILE, ARE DIM AND BLURRY; AND WHERE YOU ARE NEVER QUITE SURE WHO'S FRIEND AND WHO'S FOE. WHEN READING ABOUT IT, WE'RE VERY MUCH OUT OF OUR DEPTH AND, IN FOLLOWING BILBO'S JOURNEY, IT'S ALMOST LIKE BEING A SECOND HOBBIT, TAGGING ALONG BEHIND THORIN AND COMPANY.'

Beorn fits perfectly within John Howe's description of Wilderland because he is a being trapped between the human and animal world: at the same time, civilized and untamed, simultaneously capable of being defender or aggressor.

Tolkien was a noted scholar of the Anglo Saxon epic *Beowulf* and, in *The Hobbit*, he depicts Beorn's house (in word and picture) as being like Heorot, the long, low mead-hall of King Hrothgar that is described in *Beowulf* as 'the foremost of halls under heaven'.

Other elements of this ancient tale are reworked in *The Hobbit*, and in *The Lord of the Rings* Tolkien portrays a culture similar to that of the Anglo Saxon age in his description of the kingdom of Rohan that would provide a major design inspiration for the film sets for King Théoden's Golden Hall in *The Two Towers*.

'Having already drawn on those ideas in *Rings*,' says John, 'we didn't want to repeat them in *The Hobbit*, so we steered clear of anything too *Beowulf*-ish and headed off in a different direction – well, several different directions, because we designed Beorn's house at least five or six times!'

The final version was, in part, dictated by the location for the exterior set built in a remote valley in Paradise, near Glenorchy, on the South Island. As John explains: 'The rocks and the woodland in the area were an important factor in shaping the house so it feels very much a part of that surrounding landscape.'

Fellow Concept Artist, Alan Lee, describes the impact of seeing Beorn's house, which was built to the giant skin-changer's scale, on location: 'The effect was extraordinary, because, at a distance of a few metres, it looked as though it was a normal, human-sized building, but as you walked up to the door you felt as though you were shrinking and, because every detail of the set was so perfectly in scale, it really was like entering a giant's house.'

OPPOSITE: **Peter and Bilbo are both dressed for dinner at Beorn's house.** ABOVE: **An extraordinary, full-sized model of Beorn's house was constructed on location near Glenorchy, on New Zealand's South Island.**

That was certainly the feeling evoked in the actors playing the Dwarves, as Dean O'Gorman confirms: 'The way in which the building seemed to be morphing into the trees and rocks of the landscape gave it a very magical look, almost like a scene from *Hansel and Gretel*.'

Shortly before filming was due to commence, disaster struck. The main tree outside Beorn's house was old and, it transpired, had a shallow root bed; one night, a freak wind roared through the valley, uprooting and felling the tree. Beyond salvaging for anything other than firewood, and with the clock ticking, the Greens Department built a substitute tree, sculpted around a steel frame, dressed with moulds taken from real tree bark, dressed with leaves and moss and concreted into the ground in time for the cameras to roll. Nature's handiwork duplicated in a fraction of the time taken to create the original!

The set for the interior of Beorn's house brought its own demands and, as John Howe explains, had a highly distinctive look: 'If I had to describe Beorn's house, it would be as a Maori building built by Vikings in the Pacific Northwest of Canada: a hopefully harmonious mix of several different cultures constructed with rough building techniques.'

In terms of set construction, the Art Department's team of sculptors faced an appropriately massive challenge in taking the concept drawings, sizing them up and then building them to what had to be a colossal scale.

Although the interior of the house built by this larger-than-life character is vast and rugged, the pillars, struts and beams are all exquisitely and fantastically embellished with elaborate carvings. 'While creating the concept art,' says John, 'I surrounded myself with images of Viking art for inspiration and it was thrilling to do a drawing that was then enlarged to Beorn-scale and actually carved. Because of the size of the building, there were huge surface areas of woodwork that had to be covered with carvings and because no two were alike, every sculpted detail needed a separate drawing and had to be individually carved.'

John imagines the origins of these carvings: 'You could envisage Beorn – this rugged spirit of nature – living alone with not a lot to do, decorating his home with carved motifs and symbols of birds, beasts and plants.'

Although the designs for these decorations were inspired by the Old Norse culture of the Vikings, they were translated through the sculpting skills of New Zealander artists with a deep experience of traditional Maori carving. 'I found it really very exciting,' says John, 'seeing the designs evolve and take shape through a coming together of two vastly different cultural traditions.'

Sculpting Head of Department, Sam Genet, reveals a surprising fact about this elaborate decoration: 'However it looks to the contrary, with the exception of the tables and chairs, there's not so much as a stick of real wood in

LEFT: **How the house was built: once approved by Peter, John Howe's concept art would be coloured in Photoshop; this colour rendering would be transformed into a scale model by the Art Department, which was then scanned to produce a 3D CAD rendering; this would form the basis for the Set Builders to draw up their plans to construct the real thing. OPPOSITE: Set Decorators would complete the illusion with props such as these bee-hives.**

the place! Everything has been carved in foam polystyrene, plastered and painted with wood texturing.'

As with all the environments created for these films, it is the detail in design and the authenticity with which it is realized that carries off the illusion: woven rugs, fabrics printed with hidden birds and beasts, candlesticks, iron door hinges, handles and latches; unusual objects like bee-hives as well as everyday articles such as mugs and tableware and a range of tools and implements all built to scale to dwarf the Dwarves to a scale of just 56% of the height of Beorn.

Props Making Supervisor, Paul Gray, recalls one particular last-minute nightmare. 'I saw the drawing for Beorn's fire grate and, in my head, thought, "That's half-a-day or, at most, a day's work for the blacksmith." Almost too late, it suddenly dawns on me that this thing was around 2.5 metres across and 1.5 metres deep – and had to hold several hundred kilos of fire logs! All at once it was an entirely different story. It was a tribute to the workshop that everyone pulled together so that we somehow managed to get it out the door with half-an-hour to spare!'

The difficulty of filming scenes featuring characters of such disparate sizes required meticulous calculated accuracy on the part of the Slave Scale Motion Control cameras as MoCon Operator, Paul Maples, explains: 'The actors playing Thorin and Company are an average height of six foot; in the movie, however, the Dwarves are supposed to be around four-and-a-half feet tall while Beorn is supposed to be around eight feet, which means that Beorn is 1.77 times bigger than the Dwarves and all our calculations have to be based on that arithmetic relationship.'

In filming *The Lord of the Rings*, many of the scenes involving differences in scale – such as those in Bag End – used a vintage movie-making effect known as 'forced perspective', in which a

into a green screen cup that was set in the right place so it *looks* as if he is pouring it into Ori's cup on the big scale set. In another interesting gag, Beorn on the green-screen set, reaches past one of the Dwarf actors on the large scale set, picks up a mouse out of a little green-screen box and shows it to the Dwarves. It worked really well – except that the mouse kept trying to escape!'

On a very primal level, Beorn's house elicited a sense of wonder in everyone who visited it, of suddenly being magically reduced to the stature of a small child by the giant table and chairs. 'Because everything is larger than life,' says John Howe, 'when you are divorced from all of your usual points of contact with an environment, you become like a toddler in an adult world. It was a fascinating experience clambering up on to outsize chairs!'

All of the actors playing the Dwarves have vivid memories of Beorn's house. 'It was absolutely mesmerizing,' says Thorin's Richard Armitage, 'and everything was so oversized, we really felt as the Dwarves would have felt in that environment. I especially remember being fascinated by a beautifully carved chair with two bear heads.'

Graham McTavish, who plays Dwalin, reminisces about sitting in an enormous rocking chair: 'It was weird enough to sit in, but if you saw anybody else sitting in it, it was even stranger. It's very strange how the mind reacts: I recall looking at Ori – Adam Brown – sitting with a huge beer mug in a massive chair and being totally convinced that I was actually looking at a tiny person in a normal-sized chair.' And Adam himself recalls: 'It was just brilliant! It felt like you were in *Honey, I Shrunk the Kids*!'

Perhaps the most extreme reaction was that experienced by large-scale double, Paul Randall, who stands at 7 feet 1 inch but who was radically cut down to size in the gargantuan world of Beorn. 'For me,' he says, 'it was a new and totally unusual experience: usually, everything seems *small* to me, but not in this amazingly up-scaled house with its massive table and chairs! For the very first time in my life, I felt *small*!'

larger character such as Gandalf was placed closer to the camera than smaller characters like Bilbo and Frodo. On *The Hobbit*, such effects were ruled out. 'The reason forced perspective wouldn't work,' says Paul, 'is due to the fact that it's what's called an "in-camera trick" that basically lies about what the eye is seeing. The whole point about filming in 3D is to *show* perspective and allow the viewer to understand the depth of distance between people and objects, all of which means that forced perspective couldn't be used.'

With the Slave Scale Motion Control there are two sets: one on which the Dwarves and Bilbo are filmed among the outsize furniture and props, and another set, 400 feet away, where Mikael Persbrandt is closeted in a replica set built to what would be a normal scale for Beorn and constructed entirely out of green screen material. The action is filmed simultaneously with two cameras but the one filming Mikael has been programmed to ignore everything green and so only records the actor and his movements. The two cameras shoot in tandem, with one acting as a 'slave' and following the exact moves made by the other camera.

What is essential is that the green shapes and forms on Mikael's set simulating the real furniture and props are located in precisely the same position as the real ones in the set where the Dwarves are being filmed. Calculated by computer, the placing of those props requires mathematical precision if the two worlds are to appear in sync.

Standby Props Assistant, Grace Tye-Wood, describes how this process was used to film a couple of complicated shots: 'Beorn has a huge pitcher of milk which he pours

As with all the environments created for these films, it is the detail in design and the authenticity with which it is realized that carries off the illusion

Dave Whitehead, Sound Designer
SOUND JUDGEMENTS

'AUDIENCE RESPONSES CAN BE TRIGGERED BY A RANGE OF SOUND DESIGNS, FROM THE VERY SUBTLE TO THE OUTRAGEOUSLY RAMBUNCTIOUS.' SOUND DESIGNER, DAVE WHITEHEAD, IS DESCRIBING THE WORK DONE ON *THE HOBBIT* IN POST-PRODUCTION. 'WHILE FILM IS A VISUAL MEDIUM, IT'S STILL A FIFTY-FIFTY EXPERIENCE BETWEEN VISUALS AND SOUND. WE ADD COLOUR TO THE CINEMA EXPERIENCE. IN THE SAME WAY THAT THE DIRECTOR OF PHOTOGRAPHY ADDS LIGHT AND SHADE AND THE VISUAL EFFECTS DEPARTMENT ADDS TEXTURES, WE WRAP SOUND COLOURS AROUND THE ACTIONS AND EMOTIONS BEING PORTRAYED ON SCREEN.'

Dave is no stranger to Peter Jackson's movies and the world of Middle-earth: 'To those of us who worked on *The Lord of the Rings*, the place is now very familiar – rather like an old friend! It is ancient and fantastical, sometimes ethereal, sometimes surreal. As a sound space it can be beautiful, reverberant and lulling; and, depending on where you are in that world, either full of life or incredibly dead. Essentially, there are no rules, quite a few surprises and plenty of room for experimentation.'

Sound creation starts with early talks with the director, during which he passes on his initial ideas about the kind of sounds that he envisages for the various locations and creatures of Middle-earth. As Dave explains, that is just the beginning: 'In the finished film you have to find an almost rhythmic structure to your sound effects that will match the rhythms of the dialogue and the visuals, but it's an evolving process that goes on developing while the script, concept art and creature and set designs are refined. We try to

ABOVE: **Effects were used to deliberately heighten the otherworldly nature of certain scenes, such as during this pivotal 'Ring-world' scene between Bilbo and Gollum.** OPPOSITE: **Sound Designer Dave Whitehead hears the call of nature (*top*). James Nesbitt as Bofur sings for his supper at Rivendell (*bottom*).**

get what information we can from the different departments but, initially, we rely quite a lot on our imaginations. Every now and again we get it wrong, but most of the time we're in the ballpark and the early ideas that we sketch out give us a starting point towards where the soundtrack will eventually end up.'

A vital asset is a well-developed aural inventiveness: 'As a sound-orientated person, you have to rely on your sound memory-recall quite a lot and I tend to think in terms of "sound-a-likes", because often the best sound for a particular effect won't necessarily be the true sound made by the object, but something quite different that sounds right. You learn to be quite creative: for example, the sound made by a flickering fire can be really enhanced if you add in the sound of a flag flapping in the wind.'

The craft of sound creation remains true to the Jackson ethos that a story with a fantastical setting doesn't need to be outlandish. 'It is important,' says Dave, 'that we are grounded in the real world so that we can feel the characters' emotions and can believe that they are experiencing the things they are going through. However, it's very easy with effects to flip into the fantasy realm when we need to and the rules of realism start to disappear. So, whenever Bilbo puts on the Ring, he goes into "Ring-world" where everything is suddenly heightened and reverberant and we view it with Bilbo's strange, skewed perception.'

A film such as *The Hobbit* involving a journey requires the creation of a series of very specific and distinctive locales and the aural soundscapes are as important as the visual landscapes. Fortunately, New Zealand is able to match its glorious vistas with plenty of stunning sounds, such as those provided by the two-million-year-old Waitomo Caves used in crafting the ambience for Gollum's underground home in *An Unexpected Journey*. Having set up speakers and recording equipment in the cave, the team played a low-to-high range of sounds covering all the frequencies audible to the human ear. Recording these sounds provides 'impulse responses' – a kind of acoustic photograph of the space within the cave. 'When put through a piece of computer software,' explains Dave, 'we were able to replicate the exact reverberation of that space and apply it to the dialogue between Bilbo and Gollum in the studio so that it sounded as if the actors were in that exact cave.'

Apart from specific sound-hunting expeditions, Dave and his colleagues are constantly listening out for sounds to add to their audio library: 'Ambience plays a vital role in selling the immediacy of an environment so we recorded lots of sounds for *The Hobbit*: rivers and streams, gentle breezes and strong winds, the rustle of leaves, the buzz and chatter of insects. "Soundies", as we call ourselves, have their own kit and are constantly recording noises and sounds – much to the despair of our families and friends! If you go on a holiday, you'll take your kit and maybe record crickets whilst being savaged by mosquitoes! We are librarians of sound and gathering these things is part of our make-up; it's what we do! I really believe that the best way to design sounds for a film is to gather them yourself: knowing exactly what you need and hearing everything as it's being recorded.'

One of the best times for getting recordings that are free from extraneous sounds is at night: 'I might go out into a wood once it's dark, choose the most unkempt clump of trees I can find and record the wind in the branches; a few creaks later, I'll have

ABOVE: **A vast menagerie of animals was recorded by the Sound Department and these were combined to create the voices of the various creatures of Middle-earth. The result meant that each would sound unique, even Radagast's bird-companions.**

a component for creating an eerie forest acoustic. One stormy night we recorded in Wellington's Erskine College, a beautiful old building that was one of the locations in *The Frighteners* and is now set for demolition. We had a lot of spooky fun recording the wind howling through smashed windows and banging doors in deserted rooms.'

For Dave, there are many unique pleasures to be gained from his work: 'Our job certainly gets us off our bums and out of the studio and, at the same time, we are fortunate in experiencing beautiful Zen-like moments when we're alone with nature and reminded of just how small we are in the scheme of life.'

The sound libraries that result from these recording sessions are extensive: by the end of *The Lord of the Rings* the team had almost 600 gigabytes of sounds. 'It is our task to enhance the film with the best quality sound we can,' says Dave, 'so, where possible, we have re-recorded everything new for *The Hobbit*, although sometimes you just can't beat an old recording that simply nailed it first time around.'

In addition to all the original source sounds, the library includes examples of work by the different designers: 'We have sounds that people have augmented, stretched, reshaped, melded or morphed with other sounds. Every sound is categorized using library software with each file

having an incredibly detailed description, allowing us to do a text search across three-to-four terabytes of sounds. For example, search for "dark, steel, groan, deep" and several files would show up as being available to import into your editing software to play with.'

Nowhere is this alchemy of sound mixing more evident than in the creation of vocals for those creatures that are unique to Middle-earth. By way of illustration, here's what goes into giving Goblins their voices: 'In the first scenes where they attack, Peter said it should feel as though we were in Hell, with the howling, growling and screeching overwhelming us in chaotic anarchy. That considered, the first sounds I went for were baboons. If you've ever sat near their enclosure at a zoo, you'll know that they indulge in frequent bursts of mayhem. These frenzied vocals were perfect as a base sound and, when intermingled with camel, dog, raccoon, horse, chicken, Antarctic fur seal and human baby (with the odd sprinkling of pig throughout), we had the basic elements for our Goblins. Of course, once you get the music and dialogue into the mix – not to mention screaming bats, flaring torches, creaking wooden walkways and legions of Goblin feet with large toenail-like claws – you will scarcely hear all of the layers of sound effects that were originally created. Nevertheless, a single second of film

'I might go out into a wood once it's dark, choose the most unkempt clump of trees I can find and record the wind in the branches; a few creaks later, I'll have a component for creating an eerie forest acoustic.

could be made up of sounds recorded on several different continents which have taken people many hours to create.'

When it comes to sound effects just about any animal is fair game – and especially big game: lions, tigers and (because *The Hobbit* features the skin-changing Beorn) bears are particularly useful for creature vocals: 'Their sounds have a strong attack as well as a variety of growls that are very non-tonal and easy to shape into the mouth of an on-screen creature. But the secret is that there's always a lot more to our creatures than meets the eye – or the ear!'

The various races of Middle-earth make their own demands, such as the Dwarves. 'As soon as we knew that each of the Dwarves had their own specific weapons,' recalls Dave, 'we decided to record a huge palette of weapon sounds: swords, hammers, axes and spears. In contrast, when they sing about the Misty Mountains we enhanced the singing with the imperceptible addition of a breathy wind and the sound of smoke puffs. One of the trickiest sequences was the Dwarves' song, 'Blunt the Knives', where the first thing I had to do was find a rhythm in the effects that would segue musically into Steven Gallagher's setting of Tolkien's words. We then recorded stamping feet, cutlery *shings* and *tings* and the *chink* and *clatter* of every kind of plate, dish and bowl we could muster and edited them all into a rhythmic foot-stomping shindig!'

Post-Production Sound also relies on the talents of 'Foley artists'. Named after Jack Donovan Foley, an early Hollywood sound pioneer, Foley is the art of replacing or enhancing sounds that are generated by the characters' movement on screen such as footsteps (on a variety of terrains) for thirteen Dwarves, a hobbit and a Wizard.

'Foley artists,' says Dave, 'need to be some of the most innovative, lateral-thinking members of the sound department. Each has their own bag of tricks and props that they bring to a show and Foley adds the crisp sounds that ground a film like *The Hobbit* in a recognizable world: crunching stones under foot, a kettle being put on a stove, the rustle of an Elven robe, the clank of armour and the jangle of a horse's bridle; everything from the unfolding of a map through to Troll soup-slurps!'

In terms of magnitude and scope, the sound requirements for *The Hobbit* are comparable to those on the *Rings* trilogy but with additional challenges posed by the film's higher rate of 48 frames per second and the introduction of the innovative 'Dolby Atmos' sound format. Reflecting on the work of the sound design team, Dave Whitehead says, 'Our goal is always the same: to pair the visual resolution of the film with a matching sound fidelity. But all Peter's films challenge us in new and often unexpected ways and *The Hobbit* is certainly no exception to that rule!'

THE CALL OF THE WARG

Sound Designer, David Farmer, describes how the Wargs got their frightening calls and cries.

'They have to sound huge and threatening, so I layer several sounds together to make them as snarly and nasty as I can. We recorded lots of different dogs, looking for interesting snarls and, in the final mix, the sense of the Warg's size comes mostly from lion sounds, or one of the other big cats, and the feeling of nastiness from recordings of Rottweilers, ridgebacks and terriers.

'Peter also wanted distant wolf howls in the track to invoke that classic spooky feeling, but as soon as the camera cuts to a closer pursuit I focus the sound on something much more up-close and personal.

'Whenever there are a number of Wargs on screen at the same time I try not to use the same type of animal sound, so the moviegoer can tell one creature from another. If there's a shot where three Wargs run by and I were to use a recording of a tiger for all of them, they would all sound too similar and the listener would have to do too much work in sorting out which sound goes with each image. So, instead, I might use a wolf for one Warg, a lion for another, and a tiger for the third. That way it's much easier for them to tell which one is which.

'The pack sound of Wargs is a bit tricky: we experimented with baying hounds in pursuit of their quarry, but it usually sounds more goofy than threatening. I also have to avoid using dog-barks, as they don't quite sound as if gigantic monsters were after you. In the end, what worked best were recordings of dogs running around, playing and pulling on a rope toy: not at all scary – until *we* use it!'

MIRKWOOD

'**T**HE MIRKWOOD SET WAS REALLY SPECIAL,' SAYS ORI'S ADAM BROWN; 'THEY'D BUILT A HUGE, DARK, SCARY FOREST IN THE MIDDLE OF ONE OF THE STUDIOS. IT FELT REALLY TOXIC. I DON'T KNOW IF IT WAS A VIBE GIVEN OFF BY THE PLACE OR JUST THE SMELL OF THE PAINT, BUT IT DID FEEL LIKE WE WERE ALL GOING TO DIE IF WE WERE IN THERE TOO LONG!'

Tolkien's first description of Mirkwood – 'the greatest of the forests of the Northern world' – is far from inviting: ancient trees with huge, gnarled trunks and twisted branches swathed in ivy and hung with lichen. Standing on the edge of the forest, the way ahead appears to be no more than a narrow, gloomy tunnel winding away into the darkness. No wonder Bilbo asked if they really have to pass through such a sinister place...

Although Bilbo, Thorin and Company have no choice but to take that mysterious and menacing path, they are all too aware that, as Gandalf puts it, they have passed over 'the Edge of the Wild' and are likely to face as-yet unknown threats and terrors, as indeed they do courtesy of the labyrinthine tangle of trees and the webs of gigantic spiders. That feeling, as Production Designer Dan Hennah explains, is what the Mirkwood set was designed to evoke.

'Peter,' says Dan, 'wanted Mirkwood to have an atmosphere that would convey the bewildering effect that the place has on the travellers, causing them to disagree and argue with one another, make mistakes and, eventually, become hopelessly lost. It was rather "trippy" in a sixties kind of way and, at first glance, it might have looked as if we'd "over-tripped", because we developed a rather psychedelic look in which the trees were covered with vivid iridescent-coloured fungi and the air was heavy with mushroom spores.'

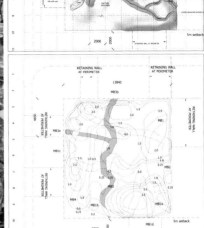

Mirkwood's hallucinogenic colour-scheme was dictated by the fact that the lighting used for the forest sequences combined with the effect of 3D and 48 frames per second will bleed out much of the colour so that, on screen, it will look far less extreme but no less weird.

It certainly made an impact on the actors playing the Dwarves. William Kircher, who plays Bifur, remembers seeing the set for the first time: 'Walking onto that set was incredible. There were greens and purples everywhere – bizarre, disturbing colours – and it was very, very creepy. It was like the films they used to show us when we were kids about what drugs can do to your head. And it was almost as if the enchantment in Mirkwood was itself a drug that was slowly eating into people so that we'd become befuddled and not quite know where we were or what we were doing. The set totally helped that feeling of disorientation, because it was so strange and otherworldly. Of course, Bifur's disorientated anyway, which doesn't help, but in that scene he's probably the most normal of them all!'

James Nesbitt, as Bofur, recalls Peter Jackson's direction of the Mirkwood scenes: 'He didn't want us totally spaced out, but was after a more subtle feeling where the mood grows increasingly eerie and we become more and more uneasy. We spent quite a few days talking the scenes through, making sure that we weren't pushing it too much,

pacing ourselves so that there was somewhere left to go with our performance when everything turns crazy and the Company is attacked and caught by the spiders.'

Because those spiders would be created later by Weta Digital, the Dwarves' side of the battle had to be fought without an arachnid in sight, as Dwalin's Graham McTavish remembers: 'The war with the imaginary spiders! There was Pete shouting out, "Okay, they're coming from that direction now… No, *behind* you! And there's another one!" So you're whipping around and he's yelling, "It's attacking you now… *Now*!" And it really reminded me of when you're a little kid and you imagine monsters; creating them in your head so vividly that you can almost see them!'

The action sequences taking place in the upper branches of Mirkwood were challenging, as Dan Hennah recalls: 'These scenes required a separate set constructed on three levels and involved major use of green screen so that digital vistas of the forest could be added later. The only

OPPOSITE: **Weta Workshop Designer Gus Hunter's concept art reveals Mirkwood's unruly tangle of root and branch.** TOP: **An enormous full-size tree-base is painted in lurid colours to combat the dampening effect of filming in 3D. To the right, set designs illustrate the complex layering of branches that will be built in the studio.** RIGHT: **Bilbo and the Dwarves re-enact the painting opposite.** OVERLEAF: **Bilbo faces up to being lost in the forest.**

physical components were the trees' branches. The set was built on three levels: at the lowest we had branches on the studio floor laid on green screen so that the actors could walk safely along them and, after the digital backgrounds have been added, it will look as if they are fifty feet up in the air. Twelve feet off the ground was a second green-screen floor with more branches, on which the stunt performers could work. Highest of all was a level of suspended branches for the exclusive use of digital actors and spiders.'

The encounter with the spiders involved numerous indignities for the actors as the Dwarves were caught in sticky cobwebs, suspended upside down and bound up with the fine silk that the creatures use to wrap their prey. William Kircher adds: 'How often does it happen in your life that you get cocooned in spider webbing? We have had some particularly interesting experiences on this film but this was one of the most bizarre: we were wrapped round and round in silicone until we were enveloped and then they sprayed more stuff on us, so it looked even better! We were wearing our prosthetics and heavy costumes so

ABOVE: **Filming in Mirkwood was as much a challenge for the actors as it was for their characters.** TOP: **Someone has left their mark at the entrance to Mirkwood; on the pillar to the left is the more formal message, written in Elvish and Dwarvish runes and Common Speech bidding travellers welcome but also warning them to hunt no game, unless they wish to 'face the wrath of the Sylvan Elves'.** OPPOSITE: **Peter can't help enjoying the Dwarves' discomfort.**

it was hot and claustrophobic. And just then – when we were completely encased – who should come on set but Peter Jackson with a big smile on his face, chuckling away, asking, "Are you alright in there?" and obviously enjoying what we were having to go through.' William laughs resignedly. 'Still, we all survived, that's the important thing.'

Strange things go on in Mirkwood and, as Dan Hennah observes, 'The place is unique and fantastic, but it's really not somewhere you'd ever want to live!'

TREE-MAKING FOR BEGINNERS

The poet Joyce Kilmer once expressed the view that 'only God can make a tree,' but that is something that the Greens Department working on *The Hobbit* disprove on a daily basis.

Landscaper, Jarl Benzon, is currently carving one of a number of trees for the Trollshaw Forest scene. 'This particular tree needs to go on a bit of a diet! It's a relatively small tree and it has too much weight in the trunk for the amount of branches.'

The tree-making process begins with an aluminium frame that is covered with polystyrene blocks to create the trunk. Any gaps are filled, the blocks melded together and the branches covered using a spray containing a building product called two-part expandable foam. It only takes a couple of minutes for the foam to set and then the real artistry begins.

'What I'm trying to do,' says Jarl, 'is make it look like a real tree, and to do that the weight of the branches needs to be correct in relation to the trunk. I love this work; I get massive joy from it! And it's incredibly special. It's more than just a job: it's work time but it's also playtime; and it's emotional; it's the best natural high I have ever experienced!' Jarl pauses in his euphoria and then adds: 'But we've got seventeen of these trees to carve by the end of the month, so I'd better get back to it!'

SPAWN OF UNGOLIANT

Giant spiders! The loathsome creatures encountered in Mirkwood are an example of a recurrent menace depicted in Tolkien's chronicles of Middle-earth. In telling Gandalf of the spiders he has seen at Rhosgobel, Radagast describes them as: 'Some kind of spawn of Ungoliant, or I'm not a Wizard.' In the Sindarin language of the Elves, Ungoliant means 'dark spider'. According to Tolkien, her descendants in Mirkwood had the power of speech; and it is Ungoliant's daughter, Shelob, that Frodo and Sam run into when they pass through Cirith Ungol on their way into Mordor.

It has been suggested that Tolkien's fascination with spiders stems from an experience he had as a small child in Bloemfontein, South Africa, when he was bitten by a tarantula. The author, however, always said that he had no

memory of the event other than of being told about it later. What is more, in a letter to the poet W.H. Auden, Tolkien wrote: 'I do not dislike spiders particularly and have no urge to kill them.' Whilst the Professor may not have disliked or feared spiders, his repeated portrayal of these monstrous beings in his books makes uneasy reading for arachnophobes!

Matt Aitken, Visual Effects Supervisor

IT'S ALL IN THE DETAIL

'IT'S THE SAME WORLD AS *THE LORD OF THE RINGS*, BUT WITH AN EXTENDED FAMILY OF CHARACTERS. YET THE WAY WE'RE APPROACHING THE WORK IS VERY DIFFERENT FROM A DECADE OR MORE AGO.' VISUAL EFFECTS SUPERVISOR, MATT AITKEN, IS TALKING ABOUT WETA DIGITAL'S INVOLVEMENT IN *THE HOBBIT*. 'BECAUSE SO MUCH OF THE FILM IS NOW BEING SHOT IN THE STUDIO AGAINST GREEN SCREEN, A GREAT DEAL MORE IS BEING CREATED AS VISUAL EFFECTS.'

Matt has worked with Peter Jackson since 1995, when he contributed digital effects to the TV 'mockumentary', *Forgotten Silver*. As well as *The Frighteners*, the *Rings* trilogy, *King Kong* and *The Lovely Bones*, Matt has helped create digital magic on such films as *Bridge to Terabithia*, *District 9* and *Avatar*.

The extent of the digital artistry in *The Hobbit* becomes clear when Matt shares a few statistics: 'What people might not realize is just how many different groups of people at Weta Digital will contribute to a single moment of film. There are some twenty eight departments and, potentially, all of them will touch that one shot. It may be just two or three seconds long, but it will involve, on average, forty to fifty people to produce the necessary visual effects.'

The fact that Weta is required to create, enhance or correct *thousands* of such shots – each filmed at 48 frames per second – demonstrates the critical importance of Weta's participation. 'We're really having to work to a whole new and extraordinarily high level of detailing,' says Matt. 'For example, you might see what looks like a simple shot of Bilbo walking past a pine tree, but it's quite possible that there was no tree there for Bilbo to walk past, in which case we have to separately model and give texture to each

individual pine-needle on every branch of that tree, because otherwise it just won't *look* like a pine tree!'

The secret of Weta's success is in paying the same exacting attention to small details as to elaborate, grandstanding set-pieces: 'We have a lot of fun with fantastic creatures such as Trolls, Goblins and Smaug the Dragon, and I think modern audiences know that there are visual effects going on when they see that kind stuff, but our greatest challenge is achieving things where people mustn't ever be aware of what we've done.'

Within the category of effects that must be so seamless as to be completely invisible to the moviegoer's eye, are what are referred to as 'cosmetic fixes', as Matt explains: 'It's more than twelve years since *The Fellowship of the Ring* was filmed and we have actors who are obviously that much older and, in some cases, are playing characters who, at the time of *The Hobbit*, are supposed to be *sixty*

RIGHT: **Making Thorin's beard appear the same throughout the first film was one of the hardest challenges faced by the Visual Effects Department.** OPPOSITE: **Complex natural phenomena, such as Rivendell's waterfalls, also demanded much of Matt Aiken and his colleagues.**

years younger than they were in *Fellowship*! So, we did a little bit of work, here and there, to mitigate some of the effects of time. It's hugely time-consuming and, because we are dealing with the features of performers, it's something about which we are very particular.'

Surprisingly perhaps, as a newcomer, Thorin Oakenshield was another candidate for 'cosmetic fixing'. At the outset, Richard Armitage wore a false beard that was part of his make-up and a few scenes were shot with him wearing it before a hiatus in filming gave him time to grow a beard of his own. 'It was a mark of how keen Richard was to really "become" the character,' says Matt, 'but, of course, the differences between each of his appearances had to be resolved. Making the two beards

indistinguishable was some of the hardest work we have done because it is subtle and has to be imperceptible.'

For Matt, one of the most rewarding areas of Weta Digital's undertakings is 'simulated work', or 'sims' as it is called for short: 'Our Effects Department is responsible for a lot of complex natural phenomena, such as the magnificent cascading waterfalls in Rivendell. These are fluid simulations requiring a lot of skill in order to make them not only appear real but – more than that – gorgeous! When Thorin and Company arrive in Rivendell for the first time, it was vitally important that the Valley of Imladris should look absolutely amazing: the sort of place you'd like to move to and where you could happily spend the rest of your life.'

THE PEN IS MIGHTIER THAN THE SWORD

'*S*MOKE-RING CONTEST AT THE GREEN DRAGON, TUESDAY.*'
GRAPHIC DESIGNER, DANIEL REEVE, IS SITTING IN AN OFFICE UNDER A WALL COVERED WITH ANNOUNCEMENTS AND ADVERTISEMENTS THAT MIGHT APPEAR ON A HOBBITON NOTICE BOARD: '*LOST: GREEN CLOAK, LAST SATURDAY, IF FOUND PLEASE RETURN TO THE IVY BUSH*' AND '*THE FINEST BEER IN THE EAST FARTHING BREWED BY THE GOLDEN PERCH AT STOCK*'.

Dan's job on *The Hobbit* (and the work he did earlier on *The Lord of the Rings*) has been a unique fulfilment of a passion that began when, aged twelve, he first read the story of Mr Baggins' journey 'There and Back Again': 'I instantly loved it and straightaway I was copying out Tolkien's runes, and Elvish script. We're talking a lifetime ago, but it's been with me ever since.'

Dan was working for a New Zealand Bank when he first heard that Peter Jackson was planning to film *The Lord of the Rings*; it seemed like an opportunity not to be missed: 'I felt sure they'd already have five hundred Elvish calligraphers working for them, but – on the off-chance – I sent in some calligraphy examples and they phoned immediately, saying, "We need to talk to you!" It turned out that

they *didn't* have five hundred Elvish calligraphers after all – in fact, they didn't have any! I was lucky in turning up at just the right moment.'

Initially, on *Rings*, Dan worked from home turning out maps, signs and documents after a hard day at the bank, but his contribution to the films was quickly noticed and helped launch his art career. Now, on *The Hobbit*, he has worked full-time for two years at the Stone Street Studios: 'The number of things I'm asked to do has expanded to fill the available time and, since I'm here *all* the time, it just goes on expanding! They keep asking, "Can we have this? Can we have that? Can you do this? Can you do that?" And I just keep saying, "Yes, yes, I can do that!" And then I figure out *how* to do it!'

A bundle of letters for the Hobbiton postman, a calendar and maps for Bag End, learned books for Rivendell, bottle labels for Thranduil's Elven wine cellar and navigation charts for Lake-town, all of which require a mastery of the various alphabets and languages of Middle-earth. 'I've been devising basic handwriting styles for the different races,' Dan explains, 'and then, within those nationalities, creating an individual distinctive look for specific characters. For example, there's a hobbit style and then there is the way in which Bilbo Baggins writes; and Dwarvish and how that language would be written by Thorin, Balin and Ori.'

This results in a great variety of lettering seen on screen ranging from our own Roman alphabet to the Runes used by the Dwarves and the Elvish script, Tengwar, which itself features variations depending on whether it is being written in Rivendell or in Mirkwood. As Dan explains, he always begins with what is to be found in the original books: 'Tolkien has given us the look of the Elvish characters and the runes, (which he, in turn, borrowed from the Norse world) but I then put my stamp on how they are written, including my choice of writing implements from quills to brushes to reed pens.'

Additionally, Dan has imagined many details about the writing habits of those peoples of Middle-earth that Tolkien never told us about, such as giving the people of Dale an

Asian-inspired calligraphy that incorporated some ideas from the Cyrillic alphabet that, over several centuries, has been used in Russia, Central Asia and Eastern Europe. Cyrillic characters were also integrated into the written language of Lake-town that has its own unique appearance: 'The form of writing in Lake-town,' says Dan, 'reflects its location and its closeness to the water. Long and thin, it is reminiscent, perhaps, of a line of docks or wharves with a suggestion of fishing paraphernalia.'

He admits that quite a lot of his work is the result of 'free-thinking' and one of the most enjoyable tasks was to create a quirky handwriting style for Radagast: 'The Wizard has his own almost indecipherable system of writing, borrowed from… well, to be honest, we don't know *where* it's borrowed from! Almost Da Vinci-esque, they are his own little untidy scrawlings and doodles — about mushrooms, butterflies and bugs, tadpoles and Lunar eclipses. He uses one or two runes that probably only he knows and there are a few characters and letters that are also glimpsed in Dale. So, like languages in our world, everything is intermixed and the result is a rich tapestry of styles and techniques that reinforces the idea that every culture in Middle-earth has its own long, intriguing, linguistic back-story.' With a laugh, Dan adds, 'I've even devised a Beginner's Guide to Orcish!'

Dan created several iconic props that play a vital part in telling the story of *The Hobbit*. The first of these, Bilbo's journal, makes its appearance in the opening moments of *An Unexpected Journey*. The journal (later referred to by

CLOCKWISE FROM OPPOSITE: **Hobbiton notices, letters for posting, a sketch of Bilbo by Ori, and pages from Bilbo's journal all reveal the invention and artistry of Graphic Designer, Daniel Reeve.**

Tolkien as 'The Red Book') was introduced in *The Lord of the Rings* and for it Dan devised Bilbo's spidery handwriting and several pages of notes and sketches.

Ten years on, the journal crossed over to provide a continuity link into *The Hobbit*, as old Bilbo begins recording his adventures for Frodo. It was a simple, effective idea but – with Ian Holm recording his Bilbo shots in London and the writing needing to be filmed in New Zealand – was immensely complicated to achieve.

'The trouble was,' says Dan, 'my hand doesn't look enough like Ian's hand to be seen writing in the journal; but, at the same time, nobody else's writing looked enough like *my* Bilbo-handwriting! Eventually, what you see on screen is made up of three separate components: wide shots from London of Ian where he's holding a quill but you can't see what he is writing, combined with shots of Ian's hand-double in New Zealand writing with the pen and my lettering appearing on the page!'

The illustration of Bilbo in his youth seen lying inside the journal when it is first opened is Dan's portrait of Martin Freeman in the role, but, although the audience isn't aware of it at the time, it is intended to be a sketch of Bilbo made by Ori, the dedicated chronicler of the Company of Dwarves. Ori carries his own notebook

BELOW: It took several attempts before the filmmakers thought Bilbo's contract was big enough. A stack of letters and replies to his party invitation, all individually crafted by Daniel, await Bilbo's attention. OPPOSITE: Thorin holds the iconic Thror's map, which would be 'magically' enhanced by Weta Digital to reveal its moon-runes. An unrolled deed proves that the Master does, indeed, own everything in Lake-town.

and, throughout the filming schedule, Dan has gradually filled its pages with further portraits of all the Dwarves and Gandalf, as well as sketches of tobacco pipes, Dwarvish carvings, musical instruments, axes, swords and assorted birds and beasts.

In Tolkien's book, Thorin quotes his terms for Bilbo's engagement as a 'burglar', including all travelling expenses and the defrayment of *funeral* expenses! In the film, these arrangements are formulated into a 'Deed of Contract', something that kept Dan occupied over many weeks: 'I started out with what was in the book – "cash on delivery, up to and not exceeding one fourteenth of total profits (if any)" – but was then asked to add a few more paragraphs, so I made another version. Next they said: "Jam in some more; smaller writing; fill up all the lines," so I did. That was version two. Then it was: "Make it even smaller, tighter; more clauses!" I did about four versions and I was still being told: "Give us more, more, more!" So I said, "Right! You want more? I'll give you more!" and the final thing just keeps going on and on, with amendments and annotations and added-on sections that fold out – more than enough to thoroughly bamboozle this poor hobbit!'

As every reader of Tolkien's book knows, the first image that you see is a map, made by Thorin's grandfather, King Thror, showing the Lonely Mountain and the Desolation of Smaug. In *The Fellowship of the Ring*, this map – badly battered – is seen framed and hanging on a wall in Bag End. For *The Hobbit*, Dan was required to recreate the map as it would have looked when Bilbo first set eyes on it: 'I

trade as fishermen. Most importantly, the chart shows Durin's Day, "the start of the Dwarves' New Year, when the last moon of Autumn and the first sun of Winter appear in the sky together", and a vital date for the Dwarves' quest, because it is on that day that the keyhole to the secret door in the side of the Lonely Mountain will be revealed.'

Talking to Dan, surrounded by brushes, pens, bottles of ink and desks littered with bundles of what look like centuries-old letters secured with sealing wax, and such intriguing oddities as a poster for Buckland's Midsummer Fayre ('Dancing, pony-rides, toffee-apples, ales and meads, fortunes told, puppets, conjurors and jugglers') it is obvious how much pleasure and pride he takes in his work. Except, as he is quick to point out, it isn't any such thing: 'I cannot call a day of this "work"! I do what I love doing – one day Orcish scribbling, another day milestones for Mirkwood with Elvish numbers; the next, a list of shaving styles for Lake-town's barbershop – and the amazing thing is people actually pay me to do it!'

had to make a map, still looking appropriately ancient, but – because this is sixty years earlier – a lot less travel-stained and battle-scarred.

Then I made a few more versions of it with increasing wear and tear until finally we were able to match the map in *Fellowship*, creating another continuity link between *Rings* and *The Hobbit*.'

The process of aging Thror's map and the other documents in the film is called 'distressing' and is as much of a craft as creating them in the first place: they are bent, folded, cockled and creased, scraped with knives, made wet, stained and dirtied, torn, ripped and even singed with fire. 'It's time-consuming,' says Dan, 'because some papers are surprisingly resistant and can often take quite a beating before showing what looks like genuine deterioration. In fact, you sometimes have to be quite brutal and deal with them in a heavy-handed manner. But, of course, you also have to know when to stop.'

For Lake-town, Dan created financial papers and ledgers for the Master's chambers and maps, marine charts, a book of herbs and ancestral portraits for Bard's house – all rendered to different scales along with a moon calendar: 'It shows the Lunar cycles, solstices and equinoxes which the people of Lake-town would have needed because of their

DOL GULDUR

AS IS TOLD IN THE WRITINGS OF J.R.R. TOLKIEN, AND WAS SEEN IN PETER JACKSON'S FILM ADAPTATION OF *THE LORD OF THE RINGS*, ALMOST THREE THOUSAND YEARS BEFORE BILBO'S ADVENTURE SAURON WAS OVERTHROWN BY THE LAST ALLIANCE OF MEN AND ELVES AND ISILDUR, THE NÚMENÓREAN MAN OF THE WEST, CUT THE RING FROM THE DARK LORD'S HAND. TWO YEARS LATER, AT THE BATTLE OF GLADDEN FIELDS, ISILDUR – THEN HIGH KING OF ARNOR AND GONDOR – WAS FLEEING AN ARMY OF ORCS. HE PUT ON THE RING TO MAKE HIMSELF INVISIBLE, BUT WHILE SWIMMING THE ANDUIN ISILDUR WAS SPOTTED BY THE ORCS AND SLAIN. THE RING LEFT HIS FINGER AND REMAINED LOST UNTIL IT WAS FOUND, YEARS LATER, BY GOLLUM.

THE OFFICIAL MOVIE GUIDE

OPPOSITE: **Concept Art Director Alan Lee's digital painting shows Dol Guldur brooding under a lowering sky.** THIS PAGE: **Gandalf discovers that this forbidding stronghold can be a very dangerous place.** OVERLEAF: **Rough stone walls bound with rusting and jagged iron: who could live in such a creepy place…?**

ABOVE & OPPOSITE: **Concept art, such as this pencil drawing by Alan Lee, was closely followed by the Set Designers.** BELOW: **The dressed courtyard set shows a statue surrounded by mysterious iron-clad niches. Concept drawings would be used by the Art Department's modellers to carve three-dimensional studies in polystyrene.**

Isildur provides a Númenórean inspiration to Alan and John's designs for Dol Guldur, as if the stronghold on 'The Hill of Sorcery' dated from a much earlier time when the island of Númenor sank into the Western sea and its people fled to Middle-earth.

'We've treated it as being an ancient place,' explains Alan, 'that might have been built by the Númenóreans and later taken over by Orcs and finally moved into by the Necromancer.'

'We always welcome any excuse,' says John, 'to add an extra layer of Middle-earth archaeology and, in *Rings*, we indulged in a bit of extrapolation in that several of the older cities and strongholds were intended to be Númenórean in design. At Dol Guldur, the result is dark, rigid and arrogant: a Cyclopean edifice built from huge blocks of stone, trussed together with iron braces that are rusting and decaying. Because the concept of riveting iron to stone (the natural being bound and held by the man-made) is so uncomfortable, the look is incredibly menacing.'

The external appearance, as Alan explains, reflects Dol Guldur's interior purpose: 'The ironwork that is helping to hold the whole place together also forms a maze of cages and dungeons and there are cavities behind this network of iron that are stuffed with skeletal human remains. The theme of entrapment follows through because Dol Guldur has been so overrun by the forest and invaded with vines and brambles so as to be virtually hidden. That was very much Peter's concept: not to have a dramatic image of an imposing, silhouetted building, such as a big, evil tower –'

'*Big evil tower?*' chips in John. 'Been there, done that!'

'– but instead,' continues Alan, 'to have a ruin that you almost come across by mistake. As if you had lost your

RIGHT: **Peter makes sure that Ian McKellen's Gandalf is sitting comfortably on his fellow Wizard's sled as he and Radagast, played by Sylvester McCoy, prepare to leave Dol Guldur.**

way in the forest and then suddenly realize that you are walking along the top of a wall or down a flight of stairs and, before you know it, are inside, drawn in against your will, trapped like an insect in a Venus flytrap.'

For John, the feeling of being ensnared is reinforced by the architecture: 'Everywhere are teeth-like spikes of rusted iron: I'm not sure when they first appeared or which of us introduced them, but they eventually became one of the key elements. The design also features a lot of over-leaning, diagonal lines and acute angles that are disturbing and oppressive; it's as if, infested by the evil that surrounds the Necromancer, the entire structure is closing in on you; and, before you know it, you are caught and unlikely to get out in one piece.'

'Essentially,' says Alan, 'our take on Dol Guldur was intended as a suitable environment for the Necromancer and his servants. One of the key sets is based on an equilateral triangle, on each side of which are three staircases. The triangle is such a great form to work with because wherever you are in the set, you've always got interesting angles and it also replicates the angle of view of a camera. You can stand in any corner, take in the whole set, and all the different shapes really play out perfectly in a wide shot. This place is going to stick in people's minds, not least because of the various implements and devices of torture and death that I invented!' Alan laughs, adding, 'I'm really not too proud of myself for some of those things and I'd rather not think about them overmuch... I just wanted to make it as creepy as possible!'

'Well, you succeeded,' says John with a smile. 'It's *extremely* creepy! Actually, Alan's really quite a creepy person, though, of course, you wouldn't immediately suspect it! Debonair, soft-spoken, well-educated, Alan Lee welcomes you to... *his dark side!'*

CLOCKWISE FROM OPPOSITE LEFT: The 'Hill of Sorcery' looms above Mirkwood; Gandalf enters Dol Guldur; evidence that prisoners have died here; a dark magic has drawn the Nazgûl to the former fortress; Radagast flees the ruins, having encountered a malevolent, shadowy presence; concept art of part of the benighted interior by John Howe and an entangled bridge by Alan Lee.

Ann Maskrey, Costume Designer
MORE THAN JUST 'SEWING'

'NEW ZEALAND IS A VERY BEAUTIFUL, BUT SOMETIMES TRICKY, PLACE.' COSTUME DESIGNER, ANN MASKREY, IS RECOLLECTING FILMING ON LOCATION FOR *THE HOBBIT*. 'THERE WERE DAYS OF GETTING UP AT FOUR IN THE MORNING, DRIVING A CAR I'D NEVER DRIVEN BEFORE TO A PLACE THAT I'D NO IDEA WHERE IT WAS. I'D BE DRIVING IN TOTAL DARKNESS, THINKING, "NO ONE'S GOT A CLUE WHERE I AM AND, WHAT'S MORE, I DON'T KNOW WHERE I AM EITHER!" THEN, THE SUN WOULD COME UP ON A BREATHTAKING VISTA SUCH AS A RAINBOW ARCHING ACROSS THE LANDSCAPE AND HITTING A DISTANT FARMHOUSE, AND I'D PULL OVER AND TAKE A PHOTOGRAPH THAT WOULDN'T LOOK OUT OF PLACE ON A CALENDAR.'

Then, within a few hours, Ann would be overseeing a baker's dozen of Dwarves being costumed and loaded into thirteen helicopters with costume assistants and their kit in order to be piloted to some remote location on the other side of a mountain range.

Whether on the road in the North and South Islands of New Zealand or in Peter Jackson's Stone Street Studios in Wellington, *The Desolation of Smaug* offered Ann a new batch of challenges and rewards to those she experienced on *An Unexpected Journey*. 'Sometimes it was simply about the numbers involved: making thirty or forty versions of Bilbo's burgundy corduroy jacket required to show various stages of wear and tear across the length of the hobbit's journey. If, for example, it is going to get covered in gloop after encountering the giant spiders in Mirkwood, you can't just throw it in the wash and expect it to look the same afterwards. And, even if you could, you *mustn't*, because you might need the gloop-covered jacket again if the filmmakers want to go back later to reshoot that scene.'

For Ann, the most exciting sequences were those where she was tackling costumes for characters previously unseen in the cinematic realm of Middle-earth, such as the Elves of

RIGHT: **Martin Freeman wears Bilbo's brushed corduroy jacket, which shows signs of wear and tear.** OPPOSITE: **Lee Pace reveals with a flourish the sumptuous purple and orange Lurex lining of his silver brocade coat.**

Thranduil to have a slightly sinister look, so I designed a brooch for him to wear at his throat that has a tendril design and, in a claw setting, a piece of mineral called iron pyrite, or Fool's Gold. Over this garment he has a robe with a massive train, and a gorgeous lining of shot purple and orange Lurex that looks like fire. The whole effect gives Thranduil a feeling of being a creature of fire and ice.'

It is a costume that actor Lee Pace inhabits immaculately: 'It has a faded grandeur but is still imposing and Lee, who is an actor with a fashion model's poise and grace – *and* great coat-hanger shoulders, as I like to call them – carries it off with drama and flourish.'

A later costume has Thranduil in a calf-length coat made from a fabric specially developed in the textile department: 'Made of silk viscose velvet, it has a screen-printed motif of a leaf pattern such as you might find on the ground at the end of autumn, when all you can see is just the veins. Sandwiched between this outer fabric and crushed velvet on the inside is a layer of silk chiffon with a tiny gold metallic stripe which, when it moves, catches a glint of light and looks particularly effective when filmed with the 3D camera.'

The woodland setting of the Elven-king's realm is reflected in many aspects of the design, such as Thranduil's rings: 'I wanted an organic look that hinted at the extent to which Mirkwood has become overgrown with suffocating vines and brambles.'

For the other new Elf, Tauriel, the forest motifs are used to help define the character's beauty: 'She has leggings of stretch velvet with a print of scattered leaves and a coat-dress that has a fitted bodice and sleeves over which she wears a corset in gilded brown Italian leather. The skirt of the coat comprises elongated, overlapping leaf shapes in a green fabric textured like tree-bark and lined with light-weight Habotai silk, mottle-dyed green and brown and with tiny fabric shapes like scraps of leaf providing a subtle texture that can be glimpsed as she moves.'

Mirkwood: 'In contrast to the Elves of Rivendell, these are hunters and warriors, beings of the forest, earthier, hardier and spikier.'

It is in Mirkwood that audiences will be reacquainted with a member of the Fellowship of the Ring, Legolas, but sixty years earlier in time and in the hitherto unseen woodland kingdom of his father, Thranduil. 'Orlando's costume as Legolas,' says Ann, 'consists of a tunic of sage green, panelled suede with cotton velveteen trousers and hand-made boots with specially sculpted bronze fastenings that match those on the leather vambraces that protect his arms when using a bow and arrow. There are added elements of decorative embroidery, inspired by the fronds of plants, over which we had to take great care, because being slightly raised, we needed to ensure that it wasn't too much for the 3D camera.'

In costuming Thranduil, Ann had the opportunity to establish a character not previously seen in *The Lord of the Rings*. 'His outfit is a fitted coat with a high collar in a fine silk brocade the colour of tarnished silver, worn with bronze-coloured trousers and handmade boots. I wanted

THE OFFICIAL MOVIE GUIDE

OPPOSITE: **Ann Maskrey's design for one of Thranduil's many outfits and the striking final costume as worn by Lee Pace. The silver tendril brooch that Thranduil wears at his throat.** RIGHT: **Beautiful but deadly: Evangeline Lilly models Tauriel's costume of a coat-dress with a fitted bodice and elongated, overlapping leaf-shapes, over which she wears a gilded leather corset, and stretch-velvet leggings.**

Ann was especially looking forward to designing costumes for Lake-town: 'It was fresh territory and I had this evocative image in my mind from the book of the cold lake with its city built on stilts. It is the only human group in the whole movie and it was such a refreshing change, after all those tall Elves and short, fat Dwarves, to be able to think: "At last, I've got some normal people to dress!"'

Peter Jackson wanted the place to be a cross-cultural melting pot of different peoples and races and that inspired Ann's designs: 'I gathered a lot of references: Tibetan, Mongolian, Russian and Afghan with a bit of Asia thrown in and then blended together – being careful to avoid the possibility of anyone saying, "Ah! I know where *that*'s come from!" Essentially, everything goes into the mixing pot, you stir it all up and, hopefully, pull out a look.'

The look that emerged is particularly suited to the climate: 'Because it's a cold place, everyone is bundled up warmly with several layers and there's a lot of fur, quilted fabrics and knitted shawls. Knowing it is also a poor community, I studied a lot of paintings and old sepia photographs of Russian peasant workers from the late nineteenth and early twentieth centuries which helped us create the feeling that Lake-town people's clothes are well-worn and have seen better days.'

Part of the look came from what Ann calls 'a simple trick' of restricting the colour palette for the Lake-town costumes: 'We avoided any and every shade of green, keeping our hues to russets, tans and mustardy tones, burgundies, purples, blues, greys and a little bit of black. Fabric decoration was in a style very different to anything else in *The Hobbit*: prints and embroidery utilizing an ethnic, tribal look. 'Lake-town is populated with people of different physical attributes, a cultural and social hotchpotch: among the crowds are adults and children, uniformed servants of the Master – even, since it is a port, a few tawdry ladies!'

The designs also evoke the fact that, whilst many of the inhabitants are lake people, there are those whose ancestors came down from the slopes of the Lonely Mountain when the city of Dale was destroyed. This suggested the idea for a cultural back-history to Lake-town that, while not specifically referenced in the film, is part of the underlying inspiration for the costume designs, as Ann explains: 'I came up with the idea of there being a Lake-town cult that developed into the concept of there being two distinct religious groupings – the blue group who worship the lake and the red group who worship the Mountain, which they believe to be a volcano.'

Lake-town's heroic central character is Bard, and – even though that heroism has yet to be fully revealed – Ann wanted him to stand out from the crowd: 'Bard has one basic costume comprising a heavy weave, dark-sand coloured, silk shirt; slightly darker loose trousers that tuck into leather-and-fur boots with an upturned toe (a feature of Lake-town footwear) and wrapping-straps. Over his shirt, Bard wears a kangaroo-hide coat – fur on the inside, skin on the outside. It looks roughly made – it's not cut on straight lines and has no finished edges – almost as though it were something that he might have put together himself.'

Because Luke Evans, playing Bard, had to film a lot of action shots under the heat of the studio lights, the costume department trimmed back the fur on the inside of the

coat to make it cooler for him to work in. However, after a couple of days' energetic stunt work, Luke went to Ann to thank her for the coat, which had afforded him some much-needed protection whilst running and leaping about on set!

Two of the most fun characters to dress in Lake-town – and the entire film – were undoubtedly the Master and his dubious servant, Alfrid, played by Stephen Fry and Ryan Gage. 'Alfrid,' says Ann, 'is dressed entirely in black but with different textures: a chevron-patterned tunic with silver fastenings under a black suede coat that is too short in the sleeve, as though it were the uniform he was given when he first entered the Master's service which he has now grown out of. To complete the ensemble, Alfrid has a black skullcap and a cape of mouldy, rotten fur. The costume is perfectly complemented by Ryan's portrayal of Alfrid's hunched body and hideous gait!'

In comparison with Alfrid's sombre costume, that of the Master is a grotesque riot of colour: 'Purple, orange, green, black, turquoise, blue and gold – you name it, it's in there! He owns some sumptuous clothes that have been completely beaten into submission and tortured beyond recognition, from the beautiful thing they used to be into something spoiled, tatty and tawdry. Under a once-beautiful burgundy leather topcoat is a waistcoat made from an antique multi-coloured embroidered sari with its threads pulled and ruined by damp and mould.'

It seems that the Master is incapable of wearing anything elegantly: from the neckband of his shirt hangs a piece of decorative lace (called a *jabot*, from the French word for a bird's croup, or craw) but the vintage piece of material is, like most of his clothes, ruined by grease and dirt. As Ann observes: 'The Master is overweight

Two of the most fun characters to dress in Lake-town – and the entire film – were undoubtedly the Master and his dubious servant, Alfrid, played by Stephen Fry and Ryan Gage.

and overblown, dirty and unkempt, utterly lacking in taste and really rather ridiculous. Hopefully Stephen Fry won't be offended if I say he pulls off that look very well!'

Despite the fact that the task of costume designer involves huge amounts of imaginative creativity and considerable experience and technical skill in instant problem-solving, Ann feels that it is a role that still doesn't have the recognition accorded other jobs in the industry: 'People think it's just sewing! Acquaintances of my mother will sometimes ask what her daughter does, and when she says I'm a costume designer, they'll often say: "Oh yes, that's nice; my daughter sews…"'

Lee Pace

THRANDUIL

'HE IS COLD AND TOUGH. TOUGH LIKE A DIAMOND.' LEE PACE IS REFLECTING ON HIS ROLE AS THRANDUIL, THE ELVEN-KING OF MIRKWOOD. 'HE IS A DARK AND TRICKY CHARACTER WHO – WHILST LOVING HIS ELVES DEEPLY – IS ALSO STRIKING AND FORMIDABLE, MERCURIAL AND MISCHIEVOUS. HE IS AN ELF WITH DUNGEONS – THAT TELLS YOU A LOT!'

At the 2003 Gotham Awards for independent films, Lee Pace won the Breakthrough Award for his performance as a transgender entertainer dating a US soldier in the docu-drama, *Soldier's Girl*, a role that also earned him a Golden Globe nomination. Other films have included *Infamous*, *The Fall*, *The Good Shepherd* and *Miss Pettigrew Lives for a Day*.

The 2004 TV comedy drama, *Wonderfalls*, brought Lee into contact with writer, Bryan Fuller, who created for him the lead role in the seven-times Emmy Award winning show, *Pushing Daisies*, about a pie-maker with the ability to bring the dead back to life.

Matters of life and death are much on his mind when reflecting on the role of Thranduil. 'One of my favourite

THE OFFICIAL MOVIE GUIDE

OPPOSITE: **Thranduil's throne started off with a modest set of Elk antlers but grew in the designs of John Howe to something more fitting the grandeur of the Elven-king.** ABOVE: **The vaulted chambers of Thranduil's realm are lit with glowing oil-filled amber lamps.** BELOW: **Lee Pace.**

things in this film,' he says, 'is the way the Elves are described as never dying. Whereas the doom of Men is that there is a finite point and purpose to their lives, the doom of the Elves is that they're immortal and live on and on through time and change. When we meet Thranduil in *The Hobbit* he is incredibly old and wise; but he is also fading.'

In developing his characterization, Lee has taken inspiration from the fact that, in Tolkien's history of Middle-earth, Mirkwood was once named Greenwood the Great. 'I'm working on the idea that there was a time when the wood was healthy and beautiful, the Elves were wise and innocent and Thranduil *was* the Greenwood. Now, however, he has become, instead, the physical embodiment of Mirkwood, allowing the hunger of greed into his heart. Although aware of it, he is incapable of overcoming it.'

Like many of the newcomers to the movie realm of Middle-earth, Lee Pace has found the creative process exhilarating: 'The most amazing part of this whole experience has been the organic way in which Peter, Fran

and Philippa work, always being open to different ideas. They're not interested in saying, "Here's your character and this is how you're going to play it." They want to know what you think and feel about the character. They want to inspire you and, when you show up on set, you have to go for it – have to really swing for the rafter – because you don't belong in this movie if you're not at least going to *try* to come up with some contribution to your character.'

Discussing Thranduil's relationship with his son, Legolas, played by Orlando Bloom, Lee says: 'I don't understand it, but even though I'm two years younger than Orlando, we really do look like father and son in a kind of weird, Elvish way. In the films, Legolas wants to break out, go into the world, engage with it and make it a better place – the ideal that will eventually lead him to become part of the Fellowship of the Ring. Thranduil, however, is more interested in holding back, letting the world do its thing and trying to preserve, in this little tiny corner of Mirkwood, what he knows and values.'

The Hobbit has given Lee a chance to create a unique characterization. 'When I am in make-up,' he says, 'with icy-grey contact lenses, a super-ashy blond wig that is rather rough and feral, and with my eyebrows lifted up to give me a nasty, numb Elvish face – I look in the mirror and see someone totally different to boring old me!'

He certainly relishes the opportunity to portray this character of power and regality, whether in Thranduil's first appearance in the film's prologue, clad in white leather amour and riding a huge white elk, or holding a sword that is a single piece of steel pierced with an Elvish motif, or passing judgement on the captured Dwarves while seated on his throne impressively dressed in a golden robe. Lee discussed the concept of his outfit with Costume Designer, Ann Maskrey, and they talked about the portraits of Louis XIV of France in which he is adorned with great ceremonial robes. 'Thranduil's is actually very simple,' says Lee. 'It's not decorative, but it *is* gold and looks incredible. This Elven-king is the money; he really dresses to impress!'

Striking though his outfit may be, Lee admits that it does have certain inherent drawbacks: 'Ask me what has been the biggest challenge in playing this role and I'd have to say that it's been walking up the stairs to my throne in the gold robe. I don't think that there is a single take where I'm not treading on it and falling over. It is less than impressive when you are trying to look calm and regal and you keep tripping on your frock!'

OPPOSITE: **From the points of his crown, to his rings and the filigree of his royal sword, everything suggests a spiky quality of thorns that tells you not to get too close to the Elven-king – or else! Even the pattern of his costume reflects the dense, twisting and tangled forms of Mirkwood.** ABOVE: **Thranduil offers a sobering welcome to his Dwarf guests.** RIGHT: **Lee Pace uses Thranduil's throne as an anchor for his character.** OVERLEAF: **The Company is led through the stunning Elven kingdom.**

NOTARY'S NOTES: THE ELVEN-KING

Movement Coach Terry Notary on Thranduil

One of the hardest things for an actor to do is to *not* try putting something on but, instead, to relax and undo all the conditioning with which we come into this world. You have to forget your humanity, let all that social conditioning dissolve away, so that you can encompass this new, nonhuman form.

It's the subtleties that I really love to work and play with. It's not about the big jumps and flights, but about those little understated moments when a character looks with knowing.

In the case of Thranduil, he's incredibly powerful and arrogant – it's like a little twist of smoke that seems to seep out of him and he has to keep this characteristic in check. I did a lot of work with Lee Pace on how Thranduil does this and we decided that he is always aware of his crown as a constant reminder of the need to control himself. There is a struggle permanently going on within him: a battle between his desire to unleash his evil side and reining himself back. He does this through the way he sits on his throne, as if the back of the throne itself acts as a restraining control, a reminder of what holds him up and what he has to uphold.

Orlando Bloom

LEGOLAS

'**I**REMEMBER SENDING PETER AN E-MAIL SAYING, "HEY, IF YOU WANT ME TO DON THE BLOND WIG AND POINTY EARS AGAIN ANYTIME, I'LL BE HAPPY TO DO SO!"' ORLANDO BLOOM IS RECALLING THE BEGINNING OF A LONG-RUNNING ON–OFF CONVERSATION THAT EVENTUALLY LED TO HIS RETURN TO MIDDLE-EARTH.

Although Legolas is not mentioned in Tolkien's book, he is the son of a character who features prominently in *The Hobbit*. In the original telling of the tale he is referred to only as the Elven-king, but in Tolkien's extended writings he is named as Thranduil. 'So, there was,' as Orlando notes, 'a legitimate reason for Legolas to appear in the films of *The Hobbit*.'

Describing Thranduil's character, Orlando says, 'He has virtually retreated from the world and is depicted as a darker Elven character whose desire for his culture's heirlooms is greater than his desire for good. Unlike Elrond, he is cool and calculating, much more Machiavellian. Lee Pace brings just the right amount of malice to the role – a kind of ethereal meanness and, in terms of our two characters, we have an archetypal king-versus-prince relationship.'

Whatever tensions exist between the two generations, Legolas clearly learns many of his father's prejudices that will manifest when he later becomes a member of the Fellowship of the Ring: 'Encountering Thorin and

OPPOSITE: **Together again after a decade: the director and the star, now accompanied by his screen father Thranduil, played by Lee Pace (*far left*). The Elf-prince in his element, on location in New Zealand's beautiful South Island (*left*).** THIS PAGE: **Orlando displays his skill with the matched pair of white knives that make Legolas such a deadly foe.**

FIGHTING THE FIVE O'CLOCK SHADOW

There are so many characters in *The Hobbit* with beards, that you might suppose that making all those hairy appendages was the biggest challenge facing the Make-up and Hair Department, but as Peter Swords King reveals, he and his team sometimes have to work hard to disguise any signs of a beard. 'Although Elves are supposed to be fair-skinned and not have any facial hair, quite a few of the actors are dark and hirsute and by the end of a day's shooting, evidence of beard growth can start coming through. Even after a quick run-over with an electric razor an actor might still have a blue shadow.'

In polite British society, at a time when men were expected to have a full beard or be clean-shaven, any afternoon evidence of beard-growth was referred to as a 'five o'clock shadow' and was considered most unsightly. Whilst nowadays, 'designer stubble' is considered cool, it remains totally unacceptable in Elvish culture! So what is the solution? '*Orange!*' says Peter. 'You just paint the beard area with orange and it totally negates the blue. Every make-up artist has a little pot of orange as part of their kit; we go around and as soon as we spot any Elves turning blue, we put a bit of orange on, blend it in with a little make-up and that'll always fix it.'

Company confirms all his preconceptions about the nature of Elves and Dwarves and corroborates the sense of history and conflict, all of which he will carry with him sixty years later. Not only that,' he jestingly adds, 'but he's slightly taller than me, which I find threatening!'

Asked whether, as an actor, he found it difficult to 'forget' the events in Legolas' future he had already played in *Rings*, Orlando responds: 'Elves live inherently in the moment – that's a major requirement in the role – therefore thinking into the future really wouldn't be very Elven!'

In *The Hobbit*, Legolas appears in a number of scenes featuring the newly created character of Tauriel. 'In many ways, I see Legolas as an older brother to Tauriel, who is spontaneous and rather reckless particularly in regard to the friendship that develops between her and Kili, so I think that Legolas is concerned for her and for how Thranduil will react, which makes it an interesting dynamic.'

Although he describes Legolas as primarily a 'physical character', Orlando has given thought to the emotional life of the Elves. 'They live for such a huge period of time,' he says, 'that I think feelings between Elves are very profound

OPPOSITE: **Legolas stands by one of the many amber lamps as he watches out for threat, both in his father's kingdom and outside, while on patrol in Mirkwood forest (top). Orlando Bloom, in full costume, appears as ageless as his character (bottom).** ABOVE: **The actor found to his delight that he was still almost as good an archer as his character.**

and run deep. After all, if you've lived for thousands of years then you know that there's no hurry, no rush!'

Since initially taking up an Elven bow twelve years ago in *The Fellowship of the Ring*, Orlando has starred in a range of films including *Ned Kelly, Troy, Kingdom of Heaven* and the first three titles in the *Pirates of the Caribbean* franchise.

Reflecting on the degree of change (or lack of it) at the Wellington headquarters of Peter Jackson's filmmaking enterprise, Orlando says: 'It was wonderful to see it all again! The studio has grown massively with bigger, better sound stages where you don't have to stop in the middle of a take for the airplanes at Wellington Airport to go over! So now it's a slightly slicker, more well-oiled machine, but with all the same charm and the same chaotic geniuses behind it!'

Returning to Middle-earth was an important and special personal experience: 'Elves are ageless in many ways and there is only really a sixty year difference between *The*

Hobbit and *The Lord of the Rings* – which in Elf terms is no time at all – so my only concern was whether the wig and costume would still fit. Fortunately they did!'

And, once back, the actor was instantly at home. 'After over a decade of living my life, it was wonderful to return to that very centred place of being Legolas. It was wonderful to connect with my inner Elf and rediscover the character's fluidity of movement, the ease and simplicity with which the Elves carry themselves. I picked up a bow again and seemed to still have what it takes, which was really cool. I loosed an arrow or two and hit a few bull's-eyes in front of thirty stunt guys, who were all sitting around waiting for me to shoot up the room, which was quite a nice, fun moment.'

Any other good things about being back? Oh, yes! Orlando has a ready answer to that question and Gimli would be proud of him: 'There's a *fantastic* amount of Orc-slaying!'

THIS PAGE & OPPOSITE: **As Captain of Thranduil's guards Tauriel reveals her deadly skill with both the short-bow and twin filigreed daggers. The designs of each weapon were conceived to extend the thorn-motif that is found in Thranduil's appearance.**

TAURIEL

'FROM WHERE I'M STANDING,' SAYS EVANGELINE LILLY, 'TAURIEL WAS AN ESSENTIAL ADDITION TO THE FILMS, AND I AM PROUD TO PLAY HER.' THE CANADIAN ACTRESS WHO BECAME KNOWN TO THE WORLD AS KATE AUSTEN IN THE CULT TV SHOW, *LOST*, AND WHO HAS STARRED IN THE FILMS *THE HURT LOCKER* AND *REAL STEEL*, IS ADAMANT THAT *THE HOBBIT* WAS IN NEED OF A LITTLE FEMININITY: 'IT IS AN ALL-BOY BOOK AND WATCHING THREE FILMS COMPLETELY DEVOID OF FEMALE ENERGY WOULD NOT ONLY BE WEARING, IT WOULD LACK A RELATABLE QUALITY. IN MIDDLE-EARTH – AS IN OUR WORLD – THERE'S BOTH SEXES, SO ADDING A FEW FEMALE CHARACTERS TO THESE FILMS WILL BRING A REFRESHING AND FAMILIAR QUALITY TO THE STORY. APART FROM WHICH, ONE CAN ONLY HANDLE SO MUCH TESTOSTERONE!'

Tauriel is head of King Thranduil's woodland guard. 'She is a trained killing machine,' says Evangeline, 'having devoted her life to the vengeance of her parents who were killed at the hands of an Orc. She moves with the stealth of a cat, is an expert with a bow and arrow and you wouldn't want to end up at the wrong end of her double daggers. She is no softy!'

As Evangeline recalls, Peter Jackson was very clear about Tauriel's combat techniques: 'Peter was adamant that no recognizable "human" fighting styles were employed. So, you won't see specific martial arts moves. Tauriel fights calmly and gracefully – but with venom. Taking on multiple enemies at once, she uses her speed, agility and knife skills to overwhelm her opponents.' And, in case this description isn't sufficient, she adds: 'Mostly, she slices them to shreds!'

The Elves encountered by Thorin and the Dwarves in Mirkwood are distinctly different from the Elves of Rivendell or Lothlórien, as the actress explains: 'Despite being shorter and smaller, there is a lethal, militarized quality to the Woodland Elves that makes them very dark and dangerous. Living in a forest that is being encroached upon by an external evil, they have closed their doors and given up on the outside world. This makes them more intolerant and less gracious than the Elves we've met in *The Lord of the Rings*. Basically, we're *scarier*!'

But there is more to Tauriel than just 'a lethal weapon', says Evangeline: 'She is young in Elf years and still holds on to the magic and excitement that was once at the heart of the Woodland people before their forest was overtaken by evil. Festive, energetic, and mischievous, they loved music, dance and drink and, more than anything, nature and the forest they inhabited. Tauriel gives us a window into that world.'

For Evangeline, being involved in the development of Tauriel's character was a new and refreshing experience: 'What was so surprising was how accessible and collaborative the writers are. Fran, Philippa and Peter seem to have no ego about what they do, they just want to get it right. They are so open to discussing your character, and welcome whatever input you

ABOVE: **Tauriel does not always share the views of her king, Thranduil.** LEFT: **The actress prepares to hit her mark.**

give. In Hollywood, that is certainly not the norm! Being part of that process makes you feel valued and gives you a powerful sense of responsibility and ownership over your character.'

There are, Evangeline points out, other significant differences between public life in Wellington and Los Angeles: 'New Zealand has been a deceiving treat. In my experience, hands down, Kiwis are the coolest people when it comes to "public figures": they have a way of recognizing you without letting that effect their behaviour. They see "celebrities" as regular people and act no differently around them than they would anybody else. It lulls you into this false sense of safety and normalcy and I don't look forward to the reality check I'm going to get when I go home.'

So, how does she feel about the long-term prospect of being globally associated with the role of Tauriel? 'I don't worry about that aspect of *The Hobbit* at all. *Lost* was a cult classic, an international hit and a favourite at the sci-fi and fantasy conventions, so I'm used to being identified with a particular character. Only in recent years have some fans started to address me on the street as Evangeline; for the most part, I've been "Kate". Being called "Tauriel" might be a refreshing change.'

Knowing the passionate nature of Tolkien fandom, and being cast as a character who is not in the original book, might have brought its own pressures, but Evangeline is unapologetic: 'Now I know the full story and trajectory of Tauriel's character, she is a very satisfying character to play. Of course, I'm well aware that there will be those who will reject her outright, others who will adore her, and every conceivable response in between; but, as an actor, you get used to that. For those watching the films, I suspect she will be the voice of the audience: putting the pieces together as they do, feeling what they're feeling, and speaking to their reactions. I think she's pretty cool!'

LEND ME YOUR EARS

'I dream about ears,' says Weta Workshop technician, Adam Kinsman, 'I really do. Actually, they're not dreams, they're nightmares!'

Adam opens the fridge door: 'This,' he says, 'is the stash!' Alongside a Gandalf nose and a loaf of bread belonging to a colleague that is past its best-before date are box upon box of gelatine ears.

One of the imperatives in creating the realm of Thranduil, King of the Wood-elves, is the maintenance of an adequate supply of Elf-ears; and the process of achieving that turns out to be more culinary than biological.

I'll explain... First, melt your gelatine at a heat of 85°C (any lower and it won't be runny enough; any higher and you'll burn it) then stir in some 'flocking', a product that adds skin-like pigmentation to the mix, and a pinch of tint to give the colouration appropriate for the character.

Next, take the two halves of a silicone mould (the 'negative' and the 'positive' that together create an Elf-ear-shaped void) and pop it into hot water to heat it up. Having carefully dried it (gelatine and water are a non-negotiable combination), grease it with spray-on cooking oil to enable the easy removal of the finished ear. Now, pour the gelatine into the negative half, making sure that it gets into every nook and cranny of the ear. Give the bottom of the mould a sharp knock to make any bubbles rise to the surface and prick them. Carefully apply the 'positive' half of the mould, squeeze the halves together, put it into what is called the 'jacket' to keep them tightly together, and apply a 5kg weight for a few minutes before placing in a freezer for an hour.

When done, open the two halves of the mould and remove your gelatine Elf-ear. Trim off any excess that has oozed out and dip it in acetone to wash off the grease and you're done. 'Voila', says Adam, 'one ear ready to be applied to an Elf.'

Demand is high: 136 pairs of ears every week during filming resulting in a total ear-output of... 'Who knows?' says Adam, 'Thousands and thousands and thousands of ears! Hence the nightmares!'

Bob Buck, Costume Designer

DRESSING MIDDLE-EARTH

'IT WAS DEFINITELY A DREAM OF MINE TO BE INVOLVED WITH *THE HOBBIT* AS WELL AS *THE LORD OF THE RINGS*, AND TO SEE BOTH TOLKIEN CLASSICS TRANSFORMED IN THEIR ENTIRETY ON TO THE BIG SCREEN.' BOB BUCK, WHO WORKED WITH ANN MASKREY AS A COSTUME DESIGNER, IS TALKING ABOUT HIS INVOLVEMENT WITH THE CINEMATIC VISUALIZATION OF MIDDLE-EARTH OVER THE PAST DECADE AND A HALF. 'THERE WAS ALWAYS A GLIMMER OF HOPE THAT, ONCE *RINGS* HAD BEEN COMPLETED, *THE HOBBIT* MIGHT ALSO BE REALIZED AND I GUESS I SET MY HEART ON BEING INVOLVED FROM THAT MOMENT.'

With the first trilogy having established such iconic images of characters and places in the minds of moviegoers the world over, it meant that, in approaching the prequel to *The Lord of the Rings*, the filmmakers had a rich legacy upon which to draw in creating the look of the new films, as Bob explains: 'The designs for *The Lord of the Rings* were definitely a jumping-off point for our return to Middle-earth. Basic design rules that had been established were now developed and expanded, whilst new rules had to be set up for the peoples and places that

OPPOSITE: With the Dwarves now clothed in oversized human garb courtesy of Bard's daughters, their hitherto strong individual colour signatures were reworked. CLOCKWISE FROM TOP LEFT: The brief for the costume worn by Thranduil when he visits Erebor was 'starlight' and 'moonlight'; the Dwarf costumes in the prologue reflect Erebor at its height; Bob's design for Beorn, which uses only natural materials as befitting the strict vegetarian; clothing worn by the Lake-town dwellers would need to be warm to combat the cold climate; a Dwarf miner wears a more utilitarian costume.

hadn't featured in the earlier films but which now needed to be visualized.'

There was also a new freedom derived from the marked difference between the style of Tolkien's storytelling in *The Hobbit* and that in his later work. 'We took what might be described as a more "fairy tale" approach, suited to the tone of the original book, and this allowed us to be a bit bolder with colour and form, making things a little wilder and more exciting; while, at the same time, being mindful of the fact that 3D and the higher film rate of forty-eight frames per second tends to show up detail while reducing the impact of colour.'

The Hobbit also provided an opportunity to explore some of Tolkien's cultures – such as the race of Dwarves, previously represented almost solely through the character of Gimli – in greater depth than had been possible in *Rings*: 'Having been closely involved,' says Bob, 'with the development of the Dwarven design aesthetic in the first three films, it was great to be able to elaborate on this and develop the design language and cultural identity to its ultimate.'

An additional opportunity to do this arose when, during 2012, a prologue to *An Unexpected Journey* went into development and Bob had the chance to work on designs for an earlier age when the Dwarven realm of Erebor was at the height of its power and glory: 'The prologue was my responsibility and it was a wonderful challenge to create costumes that helped reflect the diversity and complexity of the Dwarf kingdom and the majesty of the great city of Erebor at its height: from the lowly miner, who discovers the Arkenstone; to the mighty Thror, King Under the Mountain; his son, Thrain; along with Thorin and Balin, the young prince and the respected diplomat as they looked at the time of the attack by Smaug."

The prologue provided other pleasurable design opportunities: 'I was able to create costumes for the women and children of Erebor, which allowed me to have fun with rich and luxurious fabrics befitting the wealthiest kingdom

ABOVE: **The concept with Lake-town was that it is a cultural and ethnic melting pot, with the suggestion of a class system of merchants, servants and fisher-folk. This is reflected through choice of fabric and colour, though none is immune to the effects of the damp and dirty conditions.**

in Middle-earth. In addition to these, I was able to design Thranduil's costume as he appears when visiting the Dwarves; Philippa Boyens gave me the words "starlight" and "moonlight" as a brief and they became our inspiration as we played with texture, colour and form to create the regal attire of the King of the Elves for his first appearance on screen.'

As with everyone working on *The Hobbit*, the Costume Department had to respond to the organic way in which the films developed, so when, during the pick-up filming of 2013, flashback scenes were added to show Gandalf's first meeting with Thorin, there was a need to recreate Bree, the town of Men to the East of the Shire. 'We were designing costumes for the people of Bree some sixty years earlier than when it was seen in *The Fellowship of the Ring*, when Frodo and his companions first encountered Aragorn. During this time, Bree is still very much a crossroads town

with all kinds of folk of varying shapes and sizes passing through, and with what can best be described as a general air of dodginess! We had to create costumes from scratch for four new featured characters plus fifty extras; and because it was going to be raining (as it always seems to do in Bree), the actors could be standing under studio rain for hours at a time, so we had to make our costumes with waterproof linings in order to keep everyone dry!'

For Bob Buck, his involvement with the films carries with it a sense of fulfilment: 'I first read *The Hobbit* on moving to a strange new city, after leaving my home for the first time, and I guess I related to Bilbo's journey because I was at the beginning of an unexpected journey of my own. Working on these films, I feel as if life were now coming full circle; it has been an unbelievable privilege to be involved with helping *The Hobbit* get "there and back again"!'

LOCK, STOCK &
THIRTEEN BARRELS

'IT WAS FUN, SURREAL, AND COMPLETELY MENTAL!' DEAN O'GORMAN IS REMEMBERING BEING WEDGED IN A BARREL AND BOBBING ALONG THE PELORUS RIVER, THAT FLOWS THROUGH THE MARLBOROUGH REGION OF NEW ZEALAND'S SOUTH ISLAND, WHILE FILMING THE DWARVES ESCAPING FROM THE ELVES OF MIRKWOOD.

When, in Tolkien's novel, the Dwarves are confronted with Bilbo's rescue plan – making a getaway by means of empty wine barrels sent down the Forest River – they are less than enthusiastic: 'We shall be bruised and battered to pieces,' they complain, 'and drowned too, for certain!' Those involved in putting one of the most daring and amusing escapades in *The Hobbit* on film had similar anxieties, as Dean recalls: 'There was a slight feeling that something might just possibly go wrong at any moment, and that in itself gave us an adrenaline rush.'

In planning this key sequence, the first hurdle was finding a way to make thirteen Dwarf-filled barrels do what was required of them. 'The solution,' explains Props Making Supervisor, Paul Gray, 'was having a weighted keel: a bar was fitted under each barrel to which as many or as few weights could be attached to allow instant adjustability on site. We then provided a protective dome that screwed onto the bottom of the barrel so it wouldn't snag when going over rocks and stones on the riverbed.'

Working out how to keep the barrels upright was one thing, keeping them afloat when stuffed with costumed actors of varying girths was another. 'We tried to keep it simple,' says Paul, 'and the simple answer was inner-tubes! These provided flotation, but also protected the actors inside the

barrels. Then it was just a matter of finding inner-tubes that were the right size for the variously shaped Dwarves or modifying them to fit. For the guys involved in the research and development, who spent a lot of cold, wet time in the river, it seemed that the movie was entirely and exclusively about barrels!'

The same was true for the actors, some of whom rashly supposed that they would be spared the cold and wet, as Graham McTavish ruefully admits: 'It's a scene involving us in barrels, so of course, being an actor, you think, "That'll be the stuntmen and we'll just be in for close-ups, and thanks very much." Then Peter says, "Okay, can we

THE OFFICIAL MOVIE GUIDE

OPPOSITE: **Bilbo leads the Dwarves to what appears to be a dead end.** ABOVE: **Thorin leads his Company on the first part of their escape from the Elven-king's cellars.** RIGHT: **Martin Freeman is watered by crewmembers to save him having to get in the river for real.**

just demonstrate what the guys will be doing?" And from around the corner comes a guy in a wetsuit and a crash helmet – *a crash helmet!* – paddling a barrel, while being swept along by all this white water! And Pete says, "Uh, yeah, so that's it! Okay, let's set up to shoot." And we walk down to a little jetty like a row of condemned men and they pour freezing cold water over us – immerse us! It was like a group baptism!'

For James Nesbitt it was, nevertheless, a memorable experience: 'My favourite photograph taken of me shows me at the beginning of that first day, sitting there in my barrel with a look of pure joy on my face, because I was thinking, "This is incredible! Who in their right mind would ever come up with this, let alone ever make it happen in a way so that it could be such fun?"'

Dean O'Gorman agrees: 'Everyone was excited and invigorated. As actors, you get used to being treated with kid gloves: "Are you okay? Do you want a coffee? Do you

want water? Are you too hot, too cold?" But then this day, they said, "Just get in the barrel and then you'll sort of float, and there's a safety rope there to stop you from going further down the river, because there's a waterfall. But we think you'll be fine. Let's just shoot it!" And we loved it!'

Retained in a holding bay at one particular place in the river, the barrel-riders were released and followed the current to a point downstream where they were to be corralled and rescued. Contrary to expectations (or, perhaps, in line with them) it wasn't entirely plain sailing, as Dean reflects: 'There was a point where John Callen and William Kircher actually glided over one of the safety ropes and started drifting slowly away downriver. They were stuck in the barrels unable to do a thing. They just sat there with helpless looks on their faces drifting off into the distance.'

Fortunately, the escapees were recaptured without further mishap, but it was stressful work, especially when it came to clambering out of the barrels and splashing their

way to the shore. As Dean goes on to explain, heavy costumes, made all the heavier as a result of total immersion, turned the cast into Dwarven sponges: 'The assumption was that our fat-suits would make us quite buoyant, but the opposite was the case and we became like lead weights. I managed to get out of my barrel but I was so waterlogged that I was clambering up the embankment in slow motion.'

ABOVE: **The Dwarf actors enjoy the best theme park ride in Middle-earth!** RIGHT: **On location in the Pelorus River for the real thing.** OPPOSITE, TOP TO BOTTOM: **Peter Jackson points out the safety ropes; Aidan Turner and Adam Brown show it's barrels of fun, while William Kircher looks on; James Nesbitt invents the barrel-stroke.** OVERLEAF: **The Company of Thorin Oaken-barrel!**

ever shooting experience! It was just like being a kid again! Brilliant!'

Referred to as the 'Dwarves' washing machine', the river rapids set presented problems for, among others, the Head of Make-up and Hair, Peter Swords King: 'The fact that they were repeatedly getting dunked gave us a lot of trouble, because their wigs and beards were made of yak hair, which simply repelled the water. Of course, that's why yaks have it on their backs – so they don't get wet! But even when the Dwarves went right underwater, they still came up looking perfectly dry. So we used a special kind of gel that goes into globules like drops of water and makes the hair look wet. The next problem, however, was that because the gel is water-soluble, every time the Dwarves got re-dunked, it washed out of their hair and we had to stop and put more on to make them look wet again, while all the time knowing that the moment they *really* got wet they'd appear dry again! It was crazy: we got through pots and pots of gel, trying to make characters look wet who *were* wet but didn't *look* it!

In addition to the shots gathered on location, a river set was constructed just outside Wellington: 'It was like being on a theme park attraction,' says Jed Brophy. 'They created a river that had rapids, torrents and waterfalls. It was an amazing feat of engineering and was so convincing we didn't have to act being in a river, we were really in it and it was great fun!'

'It was the most amazing fairground ride that I'll ever go on!' enthuses Graham McTavish. 'Absolutely fabulous. We got into this circular river powered by two V8 engines – four-thousand five-hundred rpm – that shot us around this river course again and again and again! I think we completed an eighty-metre circuit in just over twenty seconds – in a barrel. I nearly came out a couple of times, others got cuts, hit their heads, banged their arms against rocks, somebody else nearly got knocked out. Pure mayhem! We went through a near-death experience, but it'll look amazing! If I had to choose, that would be the best

Peter Swords King, Make-up & Hair Designer
MAKING UP STORIES

'I'VE NEVER WORKED ON SUCH A HAIRY MOVIE!' PETER SWORDS KING, MAKE-UP AND HAIR DESIGNER, IS SURROUNDED BY SHELF UPON SHELF OF DUMMY HEADS – OR, AS THEY ARE PROPERLY CALLED, WIG-BLOCKS – EACH WEARING THE HAIR OF A PARTICULAR CHARACTER FROM *THE HOBBIT*: THE LONG, LUXURIOUS LOCKS OF AN ELF, THE BRAIDED, BEADED HAIR OF A DWARF OR THE SLIGHTLY SHAGGY CURLS OF MR BAGGINS HIMSELF.

'We've tried all the wigs on, at some point, and taken photographs: sometimes to try out different looks for characters before going to work on the actors, and sometimes just for fun (and strictly *not* for publication!), although I must admit, I thought I made quite a good Galadriel – before I grew my beard!'

Despite his jesting, Peter takes very seriously the manner in which the wigs are looked after: 'They're made of real hair and have to be treated with the same care as if they were the hair on someone's head. At the end of a day's shoot, the wigs are taken off and put onto a wig-block in order to keep their shape, using hundreds of tiny pins called 'blocking-up pins' and with tape holding down the front edge 'lace' where the wig joins the actor's forehead. The wigs are then washed, conditioned and left overnight to dry before being re-dressed in the morning for the next day's shoot.'

So where does all the wig hair come from? 'The human hair is mostly Russian,' Peter reveals; 'we use it because northern European hair is actually finer. You find the colder the climate, the finer the hair; whereas the closer you get to the equator, people's hair tends to be coarser.'

Finer hair, it seems, is better for making wigs, because the hair is knotted – a hair at a time – and with fine hair the knots are small enough not to leave any telltale evidence. 'Not only that,' adds Peter, 'but fine hair moves better, and if you are looking for wavy hair then it's easier to obtain fine hair that already has a wave, than attempting to make straight hair wavy. Essentially, we prefer to use natural hair in its natural state, because then you don't have to mess about with it and that means it always looks better.'

In addition to human hair, Peter and his team also use some animal hair, and in making the Dwarves suitably hairy, one particular species made a major contribution: '*Bos grunniens*', better known as — *the yak!* 'It was very difficult,' explains Peter, 'to get hair that was thick enough and in sufficient quantities for so many large wigs and beards; but yak hair is big and frizzy and has plenty of volume because it has a much coarser texture — something that seems not inappropriate for characters who are generally considered short, coarse people!'

Peter is a one-man authority on yak hair: 'It isn't cut from the animals, it's combed, and there are two kinds: very coarse hair off the top and what is called "belly yak", which is the hair underneath and is a little finer and softer. We've used forty kilos of yak and that is a *lot* of hair. As a result, we've pretty much decimated world supplies and there are now a great many bald yaks shivering on the mountains of Tibet!'

Although Peter worked on *The Lord of the Rings* trilogy (and has

OPPOSITE: **The wig made of fine Russian hair, as worn by Legolas, stands on its block.** THIS PAGE: **Graham McTavish as Dwalin displays the artistry of Peter's team of hair-punchers, as well as the Make-up & Hair teams' wig and prosthetics.**

an Oscar to prove it) the demands made by *The Hobbit* are considerably greater. 'Every character,' he says, 'has at least three wigs: for the actor, the stunt double and, in many cases, a taller or smaller-scale double, all of which must be made out of the same hair and look identical. That also means if a character has curly hair, then we have to make the curls on the wig worn by his small-scale double slightly tighter, so they remain in scale, which is no easy task.'

Peter's team on *Rings* numbered twenty-two, whereas on *The Hobbit* it's almost twice as many and the department has had to contend with many more tasks arising from the new improved-style silicone hobbit feet not to mention thirteen sets of Dwarf hands: 'They're like a pair of silicone gloves that make the actor's hands look slightly bigger and so help create a convincing sense of proportion for the Dwarves. Actually, they all have *two* different kinds of hands: a regular pair and another with pads on the palms for when they're holding their weapons. We had to develop these because as soon as they started swinging their swords, axes, maces and hammers around the weapons were slipping out of their hands and flying all over the place!'

In the case of one particular Dwarf, the silicone limb requirements are even more demanding: Graham McTavish's character, Dwalin, who always has his sleeves rolled up, wears an extra long pair of gloves representing not just his hands but also his arms. Like the hobbit feet, the arms and hands have to be made appropriately hairy which is, itself, an arduous task, as Peter explains: 'We have a permanent team of hair-punchers, putting hairs into the silicone – a single hair at a time – so that in any close-up shots the skin and hairs look natural and convincing. Punching hair into silicone

THE OFFICIAL MOVIE GUIDE

OPPOSITE: **Peter Swords King (top)**. **Sylvester McCoy plays the decidedly asymmetrical Radagast (bottom)**. BELOW: **Ryan Gage in the make-up chair having his 'monobrow' carefully applied.** RIGHT: **Evangeline has the seams of her glorious auburn wig touched up with gelatine to hide the join.**

hands and feet all day is, frankly, a pretty tedious job, but the results are fantastic.'

On the face of it, it might seem that the Elves would be relatively stress-free compared to the Dwarves but, says Peter, that is not the case: 'The Elves have lengthy, sleek, beautiful hair, but finding adequate supplies of extra long, straight hair wasn't easy and, as a result, quite a lot of hair-straightening goes on. It's crazy but we often find ourselves having to straighten curly hair for Elves while, at the same time, curling straight hair for Dwarves!'

It was decided that Thranduil and Legolas were to be the only really pale blonds in Mirkwood while the remaining Elves would have hair of a slightly darker hue in order to help the father and son characters really stand out from their people. 'The trouble was,' says Peter, 'we had already bought forty kilos of very blond hair! There was no alternative but to tone it down with dyes, and, believe me, dying that much hair takes a *long* time!'

Thranduil was a favourite make-up and hair subject for Peter: 'Lee Pace is a lovely, affable, gentle man but we turned him into this scary-looking character with pale skin, penetrating eyes, silver-blond hair and amazing eyebrows. He looks stunning and it is perfect for his character because Thranduil is intimidating and takes no nonsense and, let me tell you, when Lee comes on set in character, people just clear out of the way!'

Another favourite is Radagast: 'Peter Jackson wanted there to be something decidedly quirky about him, so if

you look closely, everything's asymmetrical: one side of his beard is really short, the other really long; one eyebrow and one side of his moustache twirls up, and the other side, down. He also has a prosthetic nose that was made slightly broken and twisted off to one side so as to ensure that everything about him was totally lopsided and odd.'

Another Peter Jackson suggestion was that, because Radagast is a child of nature, he should have an inhabited bird's nest in his hair and guano running down the side of his face: 'It was wonderful doing all the research and we looked at lots of different bird's nests for reference. Then, one day, Peter's son, Billy, found a nest that was perfect and that became the model for the one in Radagast's hair. All we then had to do was create a hairstyle around it that was ratty, matted and full of bird-poo.'

And, for those interested, the recipe for bird-poo is quite simple: corn flour, ordinary flour, pigment (various colours: off-white, grey and green), water and a few drops of glycerine.

Radagast may not be the most attractive-looking character, but he is a delight to behold when compared to the

ABOVE: **The Make-up & Hair team hard at work on location in the mobile Costume tent, preparing a production line of extras ready for their scene in Lake-town.**

Master of Lake-town and his odious sidekick, Alfrid: 'With those characters, Peter Jackson really stepped up the disgustingness! Take Ryan Gage who plays Alfrid: he has a truly amazing and beautiful smile – with *so many teeth!* – but we've certainly fixed that by making them look so rotten that they've turned green! We've also given him a lanky beard and hair, a single brutish eyebrow and innumerable spots and pimples as well as nasty little whiteheads in the corners of his nose – fantastically unpleasant!'

In talking about Lake-town's leader, Peter refers to the official portrait of the character displayed in the Master's Chambers. 'Alan Lee created a painting of how the Master would *like* to see himself portrayed, whereas we got on with the unpleasant business of depicting the reality! The truth, which is a far cry from the image hanging on his wall, is that he is going bald and what little hair he has is an awful gingery red, and thin, lifeless and very greasy. He has a weird little chin-beard and, while one side of his moustache is waxed and turns up, the other droops feebly down. Completing the look is a set of teeth that are bucked, crooked and filthy dirty. The final result is the vilest looking character imaginable and totally *not* how you would ever expect to see Stephen Fry!'

Perhaps the biggest day-to-day challenge has been in response to the numbers requiring make-up and hair: 'We have been working with sometimes four hundred extras a day, all of them with beards and wigs and often prosthetics, so we start our day at three-thirty a.m. in order to get everyone ready and on the set for an eight-thirty start. We stick on quite a lot of the beards using double-sided tape and we've got through over seven thousand metres of it so far – which is about the same length as twice round an average racetrack! Moustaches are not applied until the very last moment before everyone goes on set. We let the extras have their breakfast without their moustache, otherwise they get totally trashed, and when the crew are ready on set, there's a shout of, "Go moustaches!" – or "Go-mo!" for short – and then it's time for several hundred moustaches to be applied!'

Contemplating the eventual end of filming, Peter says, 'It's been a great challenge and fantastic fun, but, sometimes, just really, completely mad! The one thing I won't miss when it's over is *hair*! We're surrounded by it! We sweep it up every day, but it still gets everywhere – in your food, in your mouth, all over your clothes. I mean, I could never complain in a restaurant about having a hair in my soup because it would probably be off one of the wigs! Not only that, but when I get home my wife wants to know who the redhead is, and doesn't really believe me when I say, "Oh, no, no, darling, it's just part of my work!"'

BEARDED LADIES

A hot topic among Tolkien enthusiasts is the question of whether or not female Dwarves had beards. Whilst there is no direct answer to be found in the texts of either *The Hobbit* or *The Lord of the Rings*, there is sufficient evidence elsewhere to suggest that the females looked more than a little like their male counterparts.

When it was decided that the Prologue to *An Unexpected Journey* would feature the Dwarves of Erebor fleeing from the onslaught of Smaug, the question for the Make-up and Hair team was what sort of beards the female Dwarves would wear.

'I took a look at some of the first concept work that came through showing Dwarf women with full beards,' remembers Peter Swords King with a shudder, 'and I was saying, "*No!* It's too over-the-top, I'm just not buying this!"'

Peter spoke to his director namesake, and got approval to come up with a few looks of his own, starting with their hair. 'The Dwarves of Erebor were wealthy people, so I dressed loads of wigs, making them big, elaborate and decorated with jewels. As far as their facial hair was concerned, I knew that it couldn't be like male beards because it would simply look ridiculous. It was a crazy challenge and trying to make it work was really difficult, but I decided the beards needed to be softer and finer; so we used mohair, which is what's often used to make doll's hair and is incredibly fine. Unlike ordinary hair, it is soft and downy rather than coarse and brittle. Some of the female Dwarves have sideburns, some have chin-beards and by plaiting some of them and adding beads and gems, we created a very feminine version of a beard.'

Approval came when Peter Jackson agreed that, despite their facial hair – not to mention their larger-than-average ears and noses! – they still looked feminine. What surprised Peter Swords King was the willingness of women to don the beard!

'That was a big eye-opener,' laughs Peter. 'True, they don't look silly – actually, they're rather cute! – but I was astonished by the number of women who wanted to enlist as lady Dwarves, including Cate Blanchett!'

SERVANTS OF THE SHADOW

I N *THE LORD OF THE RINGS* TRILOGY, AUDIENCES WERE INTRODUCED TO THE GROTESQUE AND TERRIFYING ARMIES OF SAURON'S ORCS AND SARUMAN'S URUK-HAI THROUGH THE COMPELLING PHYSICAL PERFORMANCES OF ACTORS WEARING PROSTHETIC MAKE-UP CREATED BY WETA WORKSHOP. THE RESULTS WERE ASTONISHING AND MEMORABLE.

When embarking on *The Hobbit*, the initial intention was to use similar methods to create the Orc hordes that relentlessly pursue the Company of Thorin Oakenshield. Led by Richard Taylor, the talented team at Weta set out upon an intensive period of development. 'As we went into *The Hobbit*,' Richard says, 'we turned to traditional filmmaking techniques of actors in costumes and prosthetics, but with the knowledge that Peter would be taking *The Hobbit* far beyond where we had gone with *The Lord of the Rings*.' Their work, which was enhanced on set by the Prosthetic Make-up department led by Prosthetics Supervisor Tami Lane, would be used by Peter Jackson as he shot all key scenes with the cast during principal filming.

But ultimately it was agreed that the demands of shooting in 3D and 48 frames per second (with its merciless scrutiny of detail), plus the tireless ambition of a director committed to the pursuit of technical sophistication and the creation of creatures and beings beyond our imaginings, led to Weta's costumes and prosthetics being augmented and then fully replaced by digitally realized and animated characters.

'On *Rings*,' says Visual Effects Supervisor, Eric Saindon, 'Weta Workshop came up with a great many designs for Orcs that Peter really liked but which couldn't be easily realized because we knew that there would have to be a guy inside that prosthetic. This meant that we were simply limited by the physical proportions of the human body.

With *The Hobbit*, Peter wanted to take the Orc image established in *Rings* and skew it slightly to give a different look to these characters – the eyes might be further apart or the nose off from where you would expect it to be – and so accentuate the fact that they are not human.'

This has been achieved by using motion-capture in order to enable the skills of the performer to be more clearly discernible in the characterizations, as Eric explains: 'Azog, for example, was an exploration that went through a number of iterations before we reached what Peter wanted. Manu Bennett is a great actor but he's not the eight-foot tall creature that Azog is supposed to be! However, by capturing Manu's facial expressions and the nuances of his performance, we can reflect them back into his on-screen portrayal of Azog and can achieve something we could not have done if we had created him using prosthetics, which would only have given audiences a "blurred version" of what Manu conveyed with his acting.'

Whether filming in the studio or on location, the sets are 'captured' using 3D scans with LIDaR (Laser Imaging Detection and Ranging) technology that provide a digital version of the environment enabling the digital characters to be put into those environments. Nevertheless, sequences such as those in *The Desolation of Smaug* involving Orcs fighting with live actors as Elves are still challenging: 'You are severely limited by what the stunt guys representing the Orcs did on set and which then has to be digitally replaced; whereas scenes in which lots of digital Orcs interact with one another are relatively easy because we can make them do whatever we like!'

LAKE-TOWN

'IT'S DINGY, DIRTY, DAMP AND DECREPIT!' THAT'S RYAN GAGE'S VIEW OF LAKE-TOWN; HE LIVED THERE FOR WEEKS ON END PLAYING ALFRID, SIDEKICK TO THE TOWN'S MASTER, SO HE OUGHT TO KNOW. HE GOES ON: 'IT'S SINKING, IT'S DECAYING AND IT SMELLS OF SALT AND FISH. IN FACT IT *STINKS* OF FISH – *AND* PIG AND CHICKEN POO!'

J.R.R. Tolkien doesn't provide a detailed description of Lake-town beyond a drawing in *The Hobbit* that shows a collection of buildings standing on stilts in the middle of a lake. There are, however, historical precedents for settlements built on wooden piles driven into the water, most famously the city of Venice.

Concept Artist, John Howe, sees another historical link that may have helped inspire Tolkien: 'In the nineteenth century, at a time when nations were trying to find something about their past culture that was uniquely their own, the Swiss discovered remains of ancient communities along the lake shores and came up with the engaging – but erroneous – hypothesis of lake-dwellers. On an assumption that the water in the lakes was once much higher, it was thought that these villages once stood on platforms over the water. Although this idea has since been discounted, at the time Tolkien was writing *The Hobbit* it was an accepted theory that such a culture had once existed and the drawing he made of Lake-town is very much a reflection of illustrations that were being published at the time.'

This was how the visualization of Lake-town began: as a primitive Celtic-style town with thatched roofs, but as John puts it, 'the pencil sometimes wanders off to somewhere else altogether'. As a result, he and his colleague,

OPPOSITE: **Hilda Bianca, one of Lake-town's hard-working market traders.** LEFT: **Lake-town was conceived as a decaying, Middle-earth version of a wintertime Venice to reflect the icy northern clime.** ABOVE: **The enormous set was constructed outdoors and within a huge tank that could be filled with water; white paint is sprayed on to the roofs as a guide for Weta Digital to add snow in post-production. The whole set sits low in the water to show how it is slowly sinking into the lake.**

Alan Lee, soon found themselves on a journey across Middle-earth. 'It seems like familiar territory,' says John, 'but we've never been that far East or that far North before, so it was really like visiting another country. There are Russian, Finnish and Norwegian influences, but the best way to describe Lake-town is that it is rather as if Venice had been built on the lakes of Kiev.'

In his book, Tolkien indicated that there were nearby remains of an earlier settlement – 'The rotting piles of a greater town could still be seen along the shores' – and evidence of an earlier community became part of the design concept for the film.

Alan Lee explains: 'We came up with the idea of jagged stone outcrops – remnants of the earlier Lake-town, which had been destroyed by Smaug many years before – to which are attached the current wooden structures in

OPPOSITE: **A typically ramshackle fisherman's home is built to actual scale and meticulously set dressed. Almost none of the house is wood!** ABOVE: **Bard's boat edges into Lake-town.** BELOW: **Concept artists John Howe and Alan Lee prepare to make their customary cameos as members of the Master's band** (*left*). **The outlandish costume theme is also reflected in his personal guard** (*right*). OVERLEAF: **Daily life down in the under-story of Lake-town.**

a rather ramshackle fashion. Having one lot of buildings erected on top of older, ruined ones added another interesting layer of history and helped with designing what are a rather anarchic shambles of shops and houses that are really not standing up very well. Basically, Lake-town is precarious and vulnerable: the foundations are rotting away, the place is sinking into the lake – many of the gang planks are already half-underwater – and everything is leaning and listing, tipping and tilting, slanting and sloping.'

Such a complex plan presented a considerable challenge for Production Designer Dan Hennah: 'I loved the design – you could really relate to living in a town built on water where you could catch fish from the walkways or step onto a boat whenever you wished – but it was hugely problematic simply because everything is off-kilter and "wonky"; there's not a straight line in the place. Of course, it makes logical sense – the people who built Lake-town would have aimed to get it level but their efforts were constantly frustrated by a sinking pile here and a rotted timber there… But our difficulty in constructing a physical set where all the features are crooked and twisted was in trying to pass on that idea to people who have been trained in a world where floors and ceilings are horizontal, walls are vertical and the points where they meet are always at right-angles!'

Luke Evans

BARD

❧

'**M**Y FIRST EXPERIENCE OF BEING ON SET WAS BEING HOOKED UP TO A CABLE, JUMPING, SWINGING, LEAPING AND SLIDING ABOUT ON THE SNOW- AND ICE-COVERED ROOFTOPS OF LAKE-TOWN.' FOR LUKE EVANS, IT WAS AN ENERGETIC INTRODUCTION TO PLAYING THE ROLE OF BARD THE BOWMAN. 'BUT I CERTAINLY HIT THE FLOOR RUNNING AND I HAVEN'T REALLY STOPPED SINCE!'

Luke was born in Wales, a country often called the Land of Song – because its people have a natural flair for singing – and, after training at the Louise Ryan Vocal School in Cardiff, he won a scholarship to The London Studio Centre and was soon appearing in a series of West End musicals.

Garnering excellent notices for his performance in Peter Gill's play *Small Change* (one critic described him as 'a superb hunk of pent-up, incoherent longing'), led to a flurry of film roles: as the god Apollo in the 2010 re-make of *Clash of the Titans*; alongside Andy Serkis in *Sex, Drugs & Rock & Roll*, the biopic of musician Ian Drury; and as henchman to Matthew Macfadyen's Sheriff of Nottingham in *Robin Hood*. Key roles followed in *Tamara Drewe*, *Blitz* and *Flutter* before joining the cast of the 2011 version of *The Three Musketeers* to play Aramis, and going on to

portray his second Greek God, Zeus, in *The Immortals* and starring opposite John Cusack in *The Raven*.

Luke is proud of his cultural heritage, but was very surprised to receive a phone call from Philippa Boyens the night before his audition asking him to read for the role in his natural Welsh accent. The actor complied and secured the role: 'I was amazed! It's probably the biggest job I've ever done, and it's the first time I've ever been asked to use my own accent!'

If you look for detail about Bard in Tolkien's book, you will find little to go on: he is introduced just six chapters from the end of the novel, at a highly dramatic moment in the story, where he is referred to as 'the grim-voiced man' adding, in parenthesis, '(Bard was his name)'.

A few paragraphs later, Tolkien reveals that Bard is a descendent of Girion, the last Lord of Dale, who was killed when Smaug attacked the city over 170 years earlier. Luke's casting as a Welsh Bard had a wider impact on the production, as he explains: 'I didn't realize at first that my Welsh accent would mean that anybody else who was supposed to be descended from the people of Dale would have to have Welsh accents as well and that, because of the film, Dale will now be thought of as a place where people spoke with a Welsh accent!' He smiles: 'It must have been a very lovely place. I bet they sang all the time!'

A crucial task for the filmmakers was to flesh out Bard's character for the screen. This involved featuring his

LEFT: **Luke Evans relaxes on set.** OPPOSITE: **In character as the mysterious Bard.**

ABOVE: Luke poses with his screen family: John Bell and Mary & Peggy Nesbitt. RIGHT: Bard draws his great black longbow. OPPOSITE: Luke Evans in character as Bard's noble ancestor, Girion, who appears in flashback (*top*). Trying to avoid being spotted on the walkways of Lake-town (*bottom*).

family – a son, Bain (who is mentioned at the Council of Elrond in *The Fellowship of the Ring*) and two daughters named Sigrid and Tilda. 'No one talks about Bard's wife or what happened to her,' says Luke, 'but – as actors often do – I've created a whole back-story in my head which is that my wife died when Tilda was born, so the youngest child never knew her mother. To add to the sadness of the story, Bard and his poor little family – like the rest of Lake-town – live a meagre, hand-to-mouth existence. The affluent times have long gone and there's no trade and no money and not much to celebrate. Lake-town is a cold place in the middle of a lake where the best you can do is to survive. It is a state-controlled town, run by the Master, a powerful, greedy dictator, who looks after all the money and all the weaponry. Bard does his best to look after his family because they are really all he has left to live for.'

Bard's family is played by Peggy and Mary Nesbitt (daughters of James 'Bofur' Nesbitt) as Sigrid and Tilda and John Bell as Bain. For the Irish Nesbitt sisters and the Scottish-born John, the first challenge they faced was getting to grips with their 'father's' accent! 'Welsh,' says Luke, 'is not an easy accent to learn, but they've been absolutely amazing. The girls have never acted before – though, of course, they come from a strong acting background – and they've just picked it up and performed brilliantly. As for John, he's a wonderful kid and plays an integral part in the story and in my emotional journey in the film as Bard. It's a great role and John did a stellar job.'

However, being a teenager, there were issues of adolescent growth during such a lengthy shoot, as Luke explains: 'To say John grew is an understatement! He's at that age where he's growing on a daily basis. In fact, I was waiting for the day when I came in and was given platform shoes in order to work with him! One of Peter's biggest jobs is in keeping John the same height all the way through the film. Mind you, he's dealing with Dwarves, Elves, Orcs, hobbits, Wizards and Men, so 'adolescent' is just another height to add to the list. Pick-ups will be interesting and those platform shoes may come in handy yet! And, who knows, maybe by then Weta Digital will have created a new technology that can downsize a teenager.'

Having been cast as Bard and embraced the physicality of the part, Luke suddenly found himself being offered a second role when he was invited to portray Bard's ancestor, Girion, in a flashback scene. 'I think I'm one of the only people in the film who doesn't wear any prosthetics, but for Girion I was given a big false nose and a beard and got to experience what the Dwarves go through on a daily basis. I had long grey hair, a bit of a portly stomach and wrinkles on my face: I'd look in a mirror and think, "That's what I'll look like when I'm as old as my dad." It was very, very weird.'

THE OFFICIAL MOVIE GUIDE

the sun went down, people would close their doors and stay there until morning. The lake is full of ice and a bitter wind sweeps down from the Lonely Mountain. Everything is dark, damp and slightly dangerous. But the re-creation of all this was extraordinary. I'd stand in the Lake-town market square and look out at the sheets of ice and the mist of coldness rising off the water and a chill would go through me even though my brain was telling me that it wasn't real.'

Reflecting on the experience of playing a character who has been described as 'the Aragorn of *The Hobbit*', Luke sums up Bard's personality in this way: 'He's a realist and always has been. He has no reason to be anything but a realist. He never dreams. He *can't* dream. There's no way of dreaming when you live in Lake-town.'

A natural leader with a Dragon for a neighbour, Bard is forced to be a hero who, if fate dictates, may yet fulfil a legacy from the distant past. 'What's so admirable about Bard,' says Luke, 'is that he takes an immense journey, comes a long, long way, but never once loses sight of his agenda: he does what he does for his family and his people. That aim never alters, never diminishes. He really is quite a man.'

While playing Bard, the Lake-town set became a rather bizarre home-away-from-home for Luke, but, as a workplace, it was difficult to describe to friends and family: 'It reminded me slightly of what old London must have been like before the Great Fire: wooden structures with overhanging tiers so close together that the buildings on either side of the shadowy little alleys are almost touching. When

John Bell

BAIN

❝THIS IS REAL PINCH-ME STUFF! I'M THINKING: "I'M IN *THE HOBBIT*! AND THESE MOVIES WILL GO DOWN IN MOVIE HISTORY AS AMONG THE GREATEST FILMS EVER MADE!"' FIFTEEN-YEAR-OLD SCOTTISH ACTOR, JOHN BELL, IS REFLECTING ON HAVING HAD THE OPPORTUNITY TO PLAY BAIN, THE SON OF BARD THE BOWMAN. 'I GOT TO TRAVEL TO THE END OF THE WORLD AND SPEND A YEAR OF MY LIFE IN THIS MOST BEAUTIFUL COUNTRY, NEW ZEALAND, WORKING WITH PEOPLE WHO ARE AT THE TOP OF THEIR GAME, WHICH IS AWESOME. WHO WOULDN'T WANT TO DO THAT?'

John's career had an auspicious beginning in 2007 when he won a competition on the popular BBC Children's TV show, *Blue Peter*, to appear in an episode of the iconic sci-fi/fantasy, *Doctor Who*. Having attended theatre classes at the Royal Scottish Academy of Music and Drama, John secured a major role in the Irish family drama, *A Shine of Rainbows*, followed by roles in two popular TV series, *Tracy Beaker Returns* and *Life of Riley* as well as the Western mini-series *Hatfields & McCoys*, starring Kevin Costner and Bill Paxton. John flew to New Zealand accompanied by his parents. For John's father, who is a keen Tolkien enthusiast, it was an opportunity to meet the director of *The Lord of the Rings* trilogy. 'My dad is a huge Peter Jackson fan,' laughs John, 'so I really had to tell him *not* to bring his Gollum statuette in order to get Peter to sign it.'

Discussing his role as the middle child and only son of Bard, John says: 'Originally, my part was not as big, but it's kind of snowballed! Bard is quite moody and stern – in fact he's pretty much a grumpy old man – and Bain is a bit like his father, but that's balanced by a lighter, brighter, slightly smiley and cheeky side. He's really a family guy: he loves his sisters, adores and idolizes his father and will do whatever he can to help protect them.'

John is particularly pleased with the costume he got to wear: 'It was amazing; I'm wearing five or six different animals.' A fact which is confirmed by Ann Maskrey: 'Bain's coat was a fabric made in our own textile department, but the hat was fish skin, his waistcoat was calf skin, his boots were goat fur and his mittens were possum.' As John says,

enormous crane and say, "Wait! Oh, yes! I'm on a set!" So, it was great – although it did smell heavily of fish, which wasn't particularly pleasant.'

What's been the young actor's highlight in filming *The Hobbit*? 'I had the chance to do a fight sequence with Orcs! It's my favourite scene. I can remember it all and will never forget it; if someone said, "We've got to reshoot that scene," I'd go, "Right! Fine!" because I know all the choreography: throw a bench at an Orc, turn round, grab the fire poker and stab him in the shin; he swings down to chop off your head, you duck, turn around again, whack another Orc in the face, and so on. It's like remembering a dance; everyone has to work together to make it look good. I really got into it! There was rubble raining down on me, massive Orcs with blood and gore all over them and then you suddenly hear them talking in their Kiwi accents! I had such a ball that day. I loved it!'

The boy who first arrived in Wellington as the youngest member of *The Hobbit* cast is fast maturing into a young man. 'When I started,' he says, 'I was five foot one inch, now I'm five foot *seven* inches, so I've grown about six inches as well as two shoe sizes. I am the actor who's growing into their own tall scale-double! I've literally grown up in the middle of filming *The Hobbit*, and I wouldn't have had it any other way.'

'With so many animal skins and fur to keep him warm, it's unlikely Bain is a vegetarian!'

As for Lake-town, John really enjoyed working on this truly amazing set: 'It was vast: canals, buildings, little bridges connecting one part to another; a maze, a huge labyrinth with everything going every which way and dead ends all over the place. I loved those moments where you'd almost get lost: you'd forget where you were and then you'd suddenly see a camera, a giant green-screen or an

Peggy & Mary Nesbitt
SIGRID & TILDA

❧

'**W**E JUST KEPT BEING CALLED IN FOR ANOTHER DAY ON SET,' SAYS PEGGY, 'AND THEN ANOTHER DAY AND ANOTHER.'

'They started adding more scenes,' puts in Mary, and Peggy continues, 'We slowly realized, hey, this is a bit bigger than we thought it was!'

Peggy and Mary are sisters, the daughters of James Nesbitt, who plays Bofur, and his wife, actress Sonia Forbes-Adam. Sonia and the girls accompanied Jimmy when he travelled to Wellington to begin filming, but when they first heard the news that they were going to be spending a year in New Zealand, the Nesbitt sisters were not exactly overjoyed, as Peggy recalls: 'We were so angry! I was saying: "I hate you! You're ruining my life! I'm never going to forgive you!" But now I'm so happy that we came: I love New Zealand, I love going to school here and I love all the friends I've made. And *The Hobbit* has just added to the experience. It's something that we'll have with us through our whole lives.'

Around halfway through the initial period of filming, the idea arose that Peggy might play Bard's daughter: 'It

was never a plan,' she says, 'it just happened. Philippa Boyens asked me to audition and told me, 'We've got this small part. It might be fun for a couple of weeks.' I was really excited, but found the audition quite scary.'

Peggy had to read two scenes, in one of which Bard is leaving his family because he has to go away for a while. 'It was only a couple of pages,' she remembers, 'but it was very emotional. The other scene was one with all the Dwarves where I was handing out soup – something we've done quite a lot of in this film.'

'And blankets,' chips in Mary.

'Yes,' laughs Peggy, 'our main role in the movie is giving people soup and blankets!'

After her audition, Peggy was filled with doubts: 'I really thought, "I've blown it! There's no way! It's over for me!" Then, a week later, I got a call from Philippa who said, "You've got the part. It's only small, but you did really well." And from then on the role just grew and grew and grew.'

Not only that, but Peggy's sister soon got in on the act, as Mary explains: 'They thought Peggy's character, Sigrid, should have a little sister called Tilda and as we are sisters – conveniently – they thought I might as well play her. I didn't have to audition, because it wasn't really a big thing; it was going to be a tiny part, just in the background, but I was excited because I thought it would be fun for us to be in the film together. It was only supposed to be for a week or two and then we heard that they wanted us to come back the next year for pick-ups and it's just gone on getting bigger and bigger.'

LEFT: **It's a hard life for children in Lake-town, though Tilda has her ragdoll for comfort.** OPPOSITE: **The girls prepare to hand out blankets (top). Sigrid looks forward to throwing a bucket of water over Bofur (bottom).**

don't really look after Mary. There are some similarities between the characters and ourselves, but actually, as siblings, we probably spend more time annoying each other!'

One of the curious experiences for the girls has been seeing their six-foot tall father, Jimmy Nesbitt, being 'Dwarfed' as Bofur. 'I'm standing next to him,' says Mary, 'and then I'll look at him on the camera monitor and he'll look as if he's the same size as me, which is really weird, but funny as well.'

Issues of scale mean that Peggy and Mary have only ever acted with their father's small-scale double, but that hasn't stopped Jimmy from being around when they've been filming their scenes and offering some professional advice as Bofur the Impromptu Acting Coach. 'He'll watch on the monitor,' laughs Peggy, 'and then come running over in his fat suit; he'll be out of breath and he'll be saying, "Girls, you're doing good, but I've just got a few notes…" He likes to help. Except we don't always take his advice. We're like, "No, Dad! Go away! Bye!"'

With a Welsh actor, Luke Evans, playing their father, Bard's family had to speak with a similar accent. 'When we got our first script pages we learned that we were going to have to do a slightly toned-down version of a Welsh accent.' It was challenging, as Peggy admits: 'Mary and I are from South London and John Bell, who plays our brother, Bain, is Scottish, so it was new for all of us. We had dialect coaches to help us and because Luke's talking in his normal accent all the time on set, we just picked it up.'

Of Lake-town, the family's home, Peggy says: 'It's not the most glamorous of places, because it's dirty, grimy and cold.'

Not only that, but as the sisters agree their costumes are far from fashionable! 'They're not what I'd choose to wear if I was dressing casually to go out,' says Mary, 'but they *are* amazing! Peggy has a waistcoat with a pattern on the outside, but when you look on the inside there's a different pattern on the lining. You won't ever see it, but it's in there and it makes it more special!'

Talking about the bond between the sisters they play on screen and how close that is to their own experience, Peggy says: 'I think they are quite tough kids and because, in the story, our mother is dead, Sigrid and Tilda have more of a mother-daughter relationship because Sigrid really has to look after her sister; whereas in real life, obviously we have our Mum so I

As Peggy goes on to explain, there's a scene where Sigrid throws a bucket of water over Bofur. 'Even though we didn't actually get to work with each other, you can tell that I am thinking of Dad when I do it – and that I am really happy about it!'

MISS PIKELET,
DIVA OF THE PIGPEN

'**S**HE WAS BORN TO ACT,' NORI'S JED BROPHY IS TALKING ABOUT ONE OF HIS CO-STARS; 'AND, IN COMPARISON WITH HER, I FEEL LIKE A LEARNER. BUT I HAVE TO TELL YOU, HER TALENT HAS CREATED A LOT OF JEALOUSY AMONGST THE OTHER ACTORS WHO ARE NOT HAPPY ABOUT THE FACT THAT SHE REALLY STEALS THE FILM.'

'She has achieved every girl's dream,' says Steve Old, the man responsible for her casting; 'it's a classic rags-to-riches story: one day she's just an extra, the next, a star is born!' At which point it should probably be revealed that Steve's job on *The Hobbit* is Lead Animal Wrangler and that the star in question is a three-year-old native New Zealand Kunekune pig named Pikelet.

Near-sighted and food-orientated, Pikelet joined the cast along with a number of other animal extras booked for scenes in Lake-town; but fame instantly beckoned, as Steve recalls: 'We had her on set for a day and I think Peter got quite attached to her and decided to bring her into the office at lunchtime to meet Fran as his new pet. The next

thing we knew they had written a scene for Pikelet and Bofur.'

Pikelet's co-star, Jimmy Nesbitt, recalls shooting that scene: 'Frankly, she was better looked after than all of us put together, and given the full red-carpet treatment! Bofur is trying to grab some herbs that the pig is in the middle of

OPPOSITE: **Pikelet gets ready to ham it up with James Nesbitt, while Ian McKellen encounters her porky co-star at Beorn's house.**
ABOVE: **Pikelet is ready for her close-up.**

eating, but Pikelet has very particular tastes and the only way we could get her to put the stuff in her mouth was to smear it with homemade pesto!'

But that wasn't quite the end of the story, because working on a film where multiple takes are often the order of the day had its repercussions: 'After a while,' says Steve, 'Pikelet got tired of pesto and we had to try something else. Knowing that she loves yoghurt, we dipped the herbs in a mixture of yoghurt and green food colouring, which worked fine, except that the camera was really close and Pikelet was chewing away so enthusiastically that the camera lens kept getting splattered with fluorescent green yoghurt.'

In addition to her scene-stealing looks, Pikelet demonstrated a natural aptitude for a specialized branch of filmmaking, as Stunt Coordinator Glen Boswell explains: 'There was a scene where I was expecting to have to get a stunt double to stand in for Pikelet on account of her unusual size, shape and weight. But, as it turned out, she had a real talent for stunts and, whilst I think she prefers acting, I'm writing a reference for her to the union to get her on the books for stunt work. I can think of several actors around the world that Pikelet could do some doubling for!'

So, has fame changed Pikelet? Steve Old thinks she has become something of a diva: 'She's certainly enjoying the lifestyle and has become much more demanding: we have to give her more and more back rubs or she just ignores us, and she's getting quite fussy with her food: whereas we all used to pool our scraps for her and she'd be quite happy, she now turns her nose up at anything other than the very best organic fruit and vegetables. It's one of the things that comes with the territory, I guess.'

Pikelet is looking forward to spending a well-earned retirement on the estate of director, Peter Jackson, but her movie career may not be over quite yet – certainly if Jed Brophy has his way: 'She is everything I ever imagined an actress to be and let me say this, "Pikelet, if there's ever a time that you and I could do a film together, I'm up for it. Just get hold of my agent and we'll work out the details..."' Jed breaks off for a moment and then, almost overcome with emotion, adds: 'I have to admit, I'm slightly in love with you, Pikelet!'

Debbie Logan, Food Stylist

FOOD, GLORIOUS FOOD!

'ONCE THE DWARVES HAVE BEEN AT IT, A HAM IN BAG END WON'T EVER HAVE THE LOOK OF A WHOLE, PERFECTLY GLAZED HAM – HALF OF IT WILL HAVE BEEN EATEN AND IT WON'T BE NEATLY SLICED, SO MUCH AS ATTACKED AND HACKED WITH A BLUNT KNIFE!' DEBBIE LOGAN IS ABOUT TO DIVULGE SOME OF THE TRICKS OF THE TRADE OF BEING FOOD STYLIST ON *THE HOBBIT*, BEGINNING WITH THE FACT THAT AS SOON AS CHARACTERS START PICKING UP KNIVES AND FORKS, FILM CONTINUITY – AND, CONSEQUENTLY, *FOOD* CONTINUITY – BECOMES DECIDEDLY TRICKY: 'WE TAKE REGULAR PHOTOGRAPHS – ALBUMS AND ALBUMS – OF EVERY SINGLE PLATE OF FOOD IN EVERY TAKE, SO WE CAN ALWAYS RECREATE WHAT A CHARACTER WAS EATING IN ANY SHOT. AT TIMES, THIS CAN BE QUITE A MISSION, ESPECIALLY WHEN THERE ARE THIRTEEN DWARVES, A WIZARD AND A HOBBIT ROUND THE TABLE.'

In order to be able to provide sustenance for Mr Baggins' guests, Debbie had a catering unit set up as close to the Bag End set as possible, with two ovens, fridges, freezers, sinks with hot water and a large, three-tiered trolley for transporting substantial quantities of food from kitchen to table.

Debbie describes the process of producing movie food as 'developmental', a word suggesting a great deal of preparation and considerable flexibility: 'Never knowing much in advance what will be needed, I always make sure I have a hell of a lot of food ready and standing by. The food stylist's great fear is always that you'll either be asked for something that you've overlooked or for more of something that you don't have. One day, during the Dwarf feast shoot at Bag End, Peter Jackson decided the Dwarves were going to be throwing eggs around and I was calmly asked if I happened to have a hundred hard-boiled eggs!'

One of the golden rules of the food stylist's job is never throw anything away. 'The very moment you get rid of something,' laughs Debbie, 'someone will say, "What happened to that slice of pie that was on so-and-so's plate? We need it so as to be able to match with the last shot." You never assume any scene is finally done with and you never, ever, get rid of anything until you absolutely have to. There have been times when I've had to keep food considerably longer than would usually be desirable, such as a scene in Bilbo's pantry that featured some chicken bones on a shelf with fat dripping onto the floor, that had to be re-created three or four times with a month-long gap between shoots. But because it was such an important continuity detail the carcass was kept in the freezer a long way past its use-by-date – even for a prop!'

There was also a plentiful supply of cheeses: 'I had a Dutch Gouda that I bought in March 2012 and which was still in the fridge the following July, by which time it was well and truly aged! Sometimes, with less durable products, recycling is a necessity: when Balin and Dwalin are investigating the contents of Bilbo's larder

OPPOSITE: **Debbie Logan at work in her kitchen.** RIGHT: **A selection of fine cheeses on display at the Hobbiton market outside the *Green Dragon*.** BELOW: **This sumptuous feast had to be sourced, prepared and displayed at two different scales – all the while protecting it from ravening Dwarves!**

and come across something smelly that they assume to be mouldy cheese, Dwalin throws it over his shoulder. Since it was, in fact, a rather expensive New Zealand cheese called Kikorangi Blue, I had to salvage what I could between takes.'

Things often tended to get a bit messy in Bag End: 'One of my favourite items was a pretty-looking rectangular lattice tart that had a pastry base, a layer of raspberry jam and diagonal strips on top that were dusted with icing sugar. It had only been on the table a few minutes before one of the Dwarves broke it into three pieces, so it was back to the kitchen for a duplicate! On another occasion, much to my horror, Fili got up and walked the length of the table delivering beer, treading on all the food as he went. I can't quite remember how we managed to re-set the table after that, but I guess we did. At the end of such a day, I'd always have to assess what we'd lost and make sure it was replaced before the next day's shoot.'

Anything that actually had to be consumed by the cast was obviously cooked fresh, and in the case of the Dwarves' feeding frenzy in Bag End that meant a lot of food, all carefully themed, as Debbie recalls: 'Each part of the story has its unique drama, indicated by a colour palette designed by Set Decorator, Ra Vincent, that also applied to the food. So, for Bag End, we worked with earthy colours and simple, homely food. In addition to the chickens and ham hocks, there were sausages, black puddings, fruit, boiled and roasted vegetables, pies, tarts, scones and several different kinds of rustic bread, specially baked to our designs by the local baker.'

ABOVE: **Gandalf enjoys another one of Debbie's delicious cakes.** BELOW: **Beorn's honeycomb was made using a special stamp which would allow Debbie to produce it at two scales.** OPPOSITE: **Edible toffee-apples and toffee-carrots were two treats on offer to young hobbits.**

The big issue, as for so many departments on *The Hobbit*, was scale. 'Every item of food,' explains Debbie, 'had to be made twice, once at normal Dwarf scale and again as a 1.38 smaller-scale version for Gandalf. I worked out the dimensions using a pair of callipers with a pivot point in the middle so that when one end was adjusted to touch the circumference of a pie, for example, then the smaller gap at the opposite end of the callipers would indicate the circumference of the small-scale version.'

Such computations led to some amusing experiences: I spent some time in a kitchen suppliers sitting on the floor, measuring pie, cake and bun tins with my callipers until the manager finally came up to me and asked what I was doing because they'd been observing my weird activity on the store's CCTV.'

Even larger-scale issues were the order of the day at Beorn's house: 'I had difficulty getting up onto one of the outsize chairs, let alone being able to reach the table to re-set the food. Still, I made some interesting discoveries, such as the fact that if you scale up a size five chicken's egg, a size nine egg is roughly 1.38 larger; also, that a grapefruit-like fruit called a pomelo,

that's so large you can barely hold it in your hand, looks as if it's the size of an orange when it's on Beorn's table.'

Because Tolkien describes Beorn as a bee-keeper (with hives of huge bees 'bigger than hornets'), honey was clearly an essential part of the food to be offered the Dwarves: 'We got some honeycombs and I had a stamp made so I could remake the holes to a larger scale, then we broke off chunks and put them into a big bowl with several litres of runny honey and served it up with Dutch honey cake and brazil nuts.'

By far the most superior menu was that created for the luxurious Elven spread provided at Rivendell: 'The Elves are largely vegetarian,' explains Debbie, 'so there was a lot of fruit: star anise, egg-shaped red tamarillos, orangey-yellow persimmons and Cape Gooseberries with their lovely translucent skin. I produced various-coloured marbled eggs and there was salmon caviar in little boats of blanched white onion-skins decorated with pea-tendrils; parcels made out of banana leaves containing polenta; syrup cake with silver dust and pyramids of delightful little decorated sponge cakes that Gandalf had

> ## 'Every item of food had to be made twice, once at normal Dwarf scale and again as a 1.38 smaller-scale version for Gandalf.

to keep eating. Elegantly displayed on beautiful porcelain and silver swan-shaped dishes, it was a far cry from the bun-fight in Bag End!'

Inevitably, all kinds of foodie things were hardly – or *never* – seen, such as vegetables and other soup ingredients carried in the Dwarves' backpacks along with Elven *lembas* bread. There were also major food preparations for sequences that were left on the cutting room floor until rescued as part the Extended Edition DVD: 'For the Old Took's party, I cooked roast meats and vegetables with apple sauce and there was a pig on a spit-roast in the background; while at the *Green Dragon* there was a roasting goose (made of inedible silicone by the prop department to avoid having fresh meat out all day in the sun) and a lot of 'ploughman's lunches'. There were also a number of stalls, including one selling breads that, because they were only props, were baked using greater quantities of salt so they could be preserved without freezing. Another stall for the young hobbits sold boiled sweets, toffee-apples and toffee-carrots that had to be potentially edible but which, in the case of the carrots, proved amazingly difficult because getting toffee to stick to a carrot is easier said than done!'

One thing I had always to consider was the use of seasonal items, because it's all too easy to rush out and get stuff when it's on the shelves without thinking about what'll happen if you need it again in six months' time when it's no longer available. Fortunately, in most emergency situations there was the big supermarket next door to Stone Street Studios and they eventually got used to me running in the back door, saying: "Hey, can you give me two hundred bread rolls?" or "I want ten kilos of those tomatoes – no, not those, they're far too small!" Needless to say, they thought I was kind of nutty because most people went in there to buy what tasted good, I went in to buy what *looked* good!'

Life as a food stylist is anything but predictable, as Debbie admits in recounting just one bizarre happening, when else but during that Bag End Dwarf-fest: 'We were setting up the pantry for the scene where it is laden with food supplies and had almost finished when the Director of Photography came in and said, "Guess what?" It turned out the order of shooting scenes had been altered and they now wanted to film in the pantry *empty*! So we loaded the trolley back up and I kept it really close by, near the dining room part of the set. They were shooting Bilbo standing in the pantry looking astonished at the devastation wreaked by the marauding Dwarves and I suddenly noticed, there in the background, all the Dwarves sitting around the table, tucking into food – *from the trolley*! The food that I had carefully sorted, labelled and arranged for the pantry had been put on the table, dived into and ransacked! Of course, my brain was racing: the next scene was the *full* pantry and half the stuff on the trolley had gone! I rang the butcher and, mercifully, he had some scale sausages that were ready to go; so then it was back into the kitchen, crank up the ovens and spend the next couple of hours cooking, cooking, cooking!'

All in a day's work for the food stylist whose skills are more often ignored than acknowledged in the chronicles of filmmaking, but Debbie Logan knows what it costs to put on a good spread for the movies: 'I watch films and see the food and think, "Oh, my gosh! Nobody will ever realize just what's gone into that scene!" Not only that, but if you ask the average person what I do, they'll probably tell you I'm in catering!'

Stephen Fry

A MASTERCLASS IN BEING THE MASTER OF LAKE-TOWN

'LAKE-TOWN IS AN IMPORTANT LOCATION AND THE BEST WAY TO ESTABLISH IT IS THROUGH ITS MAYOR, MAGISTRATE, AND SUPREME LEADER – THE BEAUTIFUL, ELEGANT, ATTRACTIVE FIGURE OF *THE MASTER*!' THERE IS MORE THAN A TOUCH OF IRONY TO STEPHEN FRY'S DESCRIPTION OF HIS CHARACTER IN *THE DESOLATION OF SMAUG* WHO IS, IN TRUTH, A FIGURE TOTALLY LACKING IN BEAUTY AND ELEGANCE. 'ALL WE GET FROM THE BOOK REGARDING THE MASTER OF LAKE-TOWN,' EXPLAINS STEPHEN, 'IS THAT HE'S A GREEDY LOCAL POLITICIAN, AND TOLKIEN PROBABLY HAD THE SAME VIEW OF THEM AS MOST OF US, THAT THEY ARE, TO SAY THE LEAST, VENAL. SO WE BUILT ON THAT AND HAVE HIM BOSSING PEOPLE ABOUT, MAKING SUDDEN DECISIONS AND BEING RATHER MAD: A MIXTURE OF CRUELTY AND ECCENTRICITY.'

Although admittedly sketchy, Tolkien's depiction of the Master is of someone grasping, duplicitous and self-seeking, given to weasel words and putting his own interests and safety before that of the people who elected him. Indeed, when the people of Lake-town eventually discover his true nature they disrespectfully dub him 'Moneybags'.

'Yes, he's a miser,' admits Stephen. 'Money has become all he lives for, feeding on avarice. A natural hunger can be satisfied, but a miser's hunger is never satiated. He's skimmed so much off the top for so long that he now has this vast treasury of gold, but there's nowhere to spend it and nothing to do with it, so he's pathetic.'

For Stephen, the Master's authority rests on his ability to bring much-needed money into Lake-town and, in a world fraught with rival races struggling for wealth and power, to have somehow ensured a peaceful existence: 'He is a Kafka-esque master of bureaucracy with a taxation system that means if anybody who's not a citizen of Lake-town comes to visit or buy fish, they pay a little extra, which all goes into the kitty. But he has also managed to keep Lake-town free of war. Most of the population can't remember a time before the Master; and if they do, they remember the threat of Smaug.'

It is not in the Master's interests to bother the slumbering Dragon in the Lonely Mountain and, as Stephen suggests, he is less than pleased by the arrival of Thorin and his Company of Dwarves, bent on reclaiming their home and treasure: 'He's annoyed by warriors like Thorin and Bard, even the head of his guard, because they are just all about bows and arrows and swords and wanting to go off on expeditions and fight things. Of course, they're made for all this leaping-about nonsense and, I suppose, occasionally, you *need* people to leap about for you; but as far as the Master is concerned it is much better to just keep a lid on it all. His attitude is, "Give me the money and we'll sort it out, we'll keep out the Dwarves, Elves, Wizards and anybody else with ideas of going up mountains and disturbing Dragons, because nothing but harm comes of people like that!"'

For Stephen, the Master is not so much an anti-hero as just plain anti-heroic. 'His view is that warriors may be hailed as heroes and children may look up to them, but in the end the people who *should* be admired are the ones

OPPOSITE: **Stephen Fry strikes a calculating pose as the Master of Lake-town.**

ABOVE: **While nearly bursting out of his grubby outfit, the Master holds forth in his chamber. The urethane books on his shelves are as fake as his good intentions.** OPPOSITE: **In full regalia, the Master welcomes Thorin's Company to Lake-town.**

who make sure that the waterways are kept clear of rubbish, that the price of fish is kept stable and that trading with other lake towns miles away is fair and equitable. And maybe they're not heroic; they may put on a bit of weight and they may have rather unpleasant-looking scabs around the corners of their mouths, but you should thank them by not chasing off on quests for gold because it'll only bring perdition on your head. And sure enough, he's absolutely right!'

Stephen Fry has been a multi-talented media presence for more than twenty-five years. Today known as the chairman of the popular British TV panel game, *QI* (for 'Quite Interesting'), he first came to prominence in TV comedy shows, notably through Rowan Atkinson's *Blackadder* series, and his partnership with Hugh Laurie in *Jeeves and Wooster*, the BBC's dramatizations of the humorous stories of P.G. Wodehouse's stories, and the sketch show, *A Bit of Fry & Laurie*. Among his many films is *Wilde*, in which he gave a memorable portrayal of the celebrated Irish playwright, Oscar Wilde, brought to ruin through being put on trial for his homosexuality. Other roles include Inspector Thompson in *Gosford Park*; the voice of the Book in *The Hitchhiker's Guide to the Galaxy*; Gordon Deitrich in *V for Vendetta*, a role he says he took because 'I hadn't been beaten up in a movie before and I was very excited by the idea of being clubbed to death'; and Mycroft Holmes, brother of the world's most famous detective, in *Sherlock Holmes: A Game of Shadows*.

His casting in *The Hobbit* came about through his involvement with Peter Jackson's long-planned film project, *The Dam Busters*, telling the true story of the RAF's 617 Squadron that carried out strategic bombing raids on Germany's hydro-electric dams during the Second World War using the famous 'bouncing bomb'. Stephen Fry, who shares Peter's passion for Second World War aircraft and what he describes as 'perhaps the most glorious page in RAF history', was working on the development of a screenplay for *The Dam Busters* when Guillermo de Toro left *The Hobbit* and Peter decided to take up the reins.

The aviation saga had to be put on hold, but Peter told Stephen that he wanted him to play the Master of Lake-town in *The Hobbit*. 'I replied, "The Master of Lake-town?"

To which Peter responded, "No, you won't remember him, but believe me, people who watch the film will.'"

Talking about Lake-town and its Master, Peter Jackson says: 'It's amazing how little time is spent in Lake-town in Tolkien's book. We wanted the place to have greater weight in the narrative of the film, so we have expanded that part of Tolkien's world in order to give it and the characters there greater value, so that when Smaug attacks they are more anchored in the story. I really didn't want Stephen to be recognized from the roles he has played in the past; I wanted him to be a 'Les Patterson' version of Stephen Fry. He certainly rose to the occasion and has created a really interesting, very grotesque character for the Master.'

Stephen agrees: 'He doesn't stack up much, the Master, it must be said. Unlike characters such as Legolas, who blithely leaps around like a bloody gazelle all the time shooting people with his blasted arrows and looking cute, the Master is a repulsive and faintly comic figure.'

A suitably repellent look was devised: straggly ginger hair, combed across to disguise the fact that it is badly thinning, and what Stephen describes as 'a rather melancholy wispy beard'. That, however, was just the beginning: 'He's got gruesome teeth, broken skin with awful capillaries and bits of psoriasis in his beard that probably, in close-up, are all-too visible. I began to get the impression that the character was giving Peter a chance to exercise his love of the macabre and pour all his old splat-tastic talents – going back to *Brain Dead* and *Bud Taste* – into this visualization of the Master.'

A further unpleasant trait was added with Stephen's suggestion that the Master suffered with a severe case of acid reflux. 'Peter found that very amusing and so he has to keep saying, "Excuse me," because he just stuffs things into his mouth and pours down liquids without thinking about his digestion; as a result, he's screwed as far as his alimentary canal is concerned.'

The Master's once-beautiful clothes also underwent brutalization: 'The costumes were joyous: like a combination of Cossack, Uzbeki and Klingon and yet, somehow, marvellously all their own. They were grand and gorgeous – the most amazingly beautiful brocades and velvets you've ever seen. Stunning! But since they are essentially 'clothes' not 'costumes' and because the people of Lake-town live in a damp, smelly, fish-infested, wooden city that's been unchanged since Smaug the Dragon moved into the Mountain, everything's in a mess and a state. So, the Master's velvet is now moth-eaten, the plush is worn, and because he's a messy eater and has dropped food all over himself, everything is spoiled and stained.'

The Lake-town set, says Stephen, showed a similar level of distress and degradation: 'It's wonderfully drippy and mouldy with bits of grass growing out of the cobbles and, like every location in the film, looking as if it's been there for hundreds of years. Nevertheless, there are still a few surviving vestiges of an earlier, more prosperous, era: 'The Master is very well served by the relics of his youth, which litter Lake-town, such as his official portrait where he stands proudly in younger, better days. I think at some point he was a very charismatic figure who either through intelligence, natural cunning or generalship got himself elected. The other is the prow of his barge that has an idealized likeness of him as a noble man with flowing golden hair looking out over the waters.'

Turning to the Master's relationship with his attendant, Alfrid, Stephen says: 'I think they've developed a bizarre symbiosis where they need each other. Alfrid was probably an orphaned kitchen boy who taught himself to read and was spotted by the Master, who thought he could use someone like that; and the rather greedy and cowardly Alfrid is quite content to empty the Master's chamber pot out of the window without being revolted by the contents, while looking forward to the day he might eventually take over from him...'

THE MAKING OF A MASTER-PIECE

'LIKE A LOT OF IDEAS, THE PORTRAIT STARTED AS A LOOSELY SKETCHED AFTERTHOUGHT IN A DRAWING OF THE SET FOR THE MASTER'S BEDCHAMBER.' ALAN LEE IS REVEALING THE SECRETS BEHIND THE MASTER OF LAKE-TOWN'S PORTRAIT.

'There was no mention of it in the script, but the notion that there was a canvas on the wall, which I thought could be a portrait of the Master, stuck, and eventually made it onto Prop Master Nick Weir's list of objects to be sourced or created.

'As the character of the Master developed into a vain and corrupt individual who clearly saw himself as a handsome, wealthy and cultivated paragon of worthiness, there was an opportunity to exemplify that in the portrait. I did

a pencil sketch for Peter to which he responded well, asking that the painting be larger-than-life size.

'Stephen Fry was having a costume fitting soon after he arrived for the first time, and Director of Photography, Andrew Lesnie, arranged a lighting set-up with a grey paper backdrop so we could shoot some photos. We quickly established the pose and Stephen modelled the ornate and beautifully made costume. We wanted him to look proud, puffed up and totally in love with himself.

ABOVE: **The Master's portrait is the cleanest thing in his bed-chamber.** OPPOSITE: **Alan Lee's original sketch** (*top*). **Peter Jackson unveils the Master's portrait and Stephen Fry is (almost) lost for words** (*bottom*).

Then I worked up the best image in Photoshop, making the face and hands less photographic, adding flowing hair and a beard and moustache, and painted him against an appropriate background with drapery and a view through a window over his domain. I added a marble bust of a philosopher on a pedestal that I thought would add a touch of gravitas, but half-obscured it with the Master's out-thrust elbow to emphasize his need to upstage everyone around him! Peter saw it as a work in progress and asked for the hair to be even more luxuriant and flowing!

'Nick Weir found a company that printed photographs onto canvas and in the meantime started work on sculpting a suitably ornate frame. When the prints came back, one of them was stretched on a wooden frame and what it then needed was a texture that would make it look like an oil painting. Kathryn Lim, Head of the Painting and Set-finishing Department, and I applied a thick coat of varnish over the surface and textured it with bristle brushes. It looked good, but was still too much like a photograph; so, when it had dried, we painted over most of the surface again in acrylic – adding extra highlights to the pearls and gold buttons to increase the "bling effect" – followed by a last coat of varnish to pull the whole thing together. Finally, Kathryn's team painted, gold-foiled and aged the frame – not forgetting to age the back of the painting, just in case it would be seen from behind.

The bedchamber set was exquisitely dressed and finished, thanks to Set Decorator, Ra Vincent, and his team, and the painting looked great when it was hung on the wall, providing a wonderful contrast to the bedraggled, seedy looking Master as he is woken up by his equally dishevelled servant, Alfrid.

What began as an inconsequential sketch ended up as a major prop in the film and the painting was such a success that it inspired the pose of the sculpted figurehead on the prow of the Master's barge.

It may not be a pretty face, but it's succeeded in launching at least one ship!

Ryan Gage

ALFRID

———————⬥———————

'I AM A VALET, WAITER, POLITICAL ADVISOR AND GENERAL DOGSBODY.' RYAN GAGE IS CATALOGUING ALFRID'S DUTIES IN THE SERVICE OF THE MASTER OF LAKE-TOWN. 'I OVERSEE THE COLLECTION OF TOLLS AND TAXES, DO THE BOOKKEEPING AND EMPTY HIS CHAMBER POT. I'M SIMPLY THE MASTER'S MANSERVANT AND BITCH. BASICALLY, I'M HIS BITCH!'

In his first major film role, Ryan plays a character that some will be quick to say is not in Tolkien's book. 'Wrong!' says the actor. 'There is one mention of him, not by name, but Tolkien writes about "The Master and his councillors". True, it says "councillors", plural, but we just have the one – *me* – and I counsel! So, I'm legitimate! Alfrid is useful because there's not a great deal of dialogue in the Lake-town passages in *The Hobbit*, so rather than having the Master sitting in his room on his own, planning and conniving, it's more interesting to have him interacting with another character and speaking his thoughts aloud to someone who's a living, breathing individual with his own journey in the story.'

That character, however, was not the role Ryan was originally offered. After an initial video audition, in which he tried out for the part of Alfrid, Ryan got to meet with Peter, Fran and Philippa in London. It was a curious event at which he read for various roles including one of the Dwarves: 'I think it was Jimmy's Dwarf,' he says, referring to Bofur, 'so I didn't have a chance!' In a moment of sheer madness, or pure inspiration, Ryan decided to have a bit of fun by staging an impromptu *Hobbit* quiz, in which he asked the trio of producers a series of really hard questions. 'For some reason, I just thought that was a funny idea and they laughed. Then I started asking my questions. They were completely arbitrary and impossible. I'd just plucked them out of the book and, of course, *I* didn't know any of the answers. The casting directors are looking at me like, "What are you *doing*?" But Peter, Fran and Philippa were really going for it as if they were on some game show that they'd been playing for several weeks with a huge cash prize at the end of it. Suddenly it was getting a bit serious and there wasn't any more laughing.'

After the quiz, which had rather tested the memories of Ryan's three 'contestants', he completed his audition and left feeling somewhat uncertain about what he had done. 'I went home,' he recalls, 'and I said to my friends, "I think I've just thrown away my audition for *The Hobbit*, totally blown it by being silly." I thought they would have to be very thick-skinned people to want to employ me after doing that. But fortunately they took it with great good humour and when I got a call from Fran and Philippa telling me that they wanted me in the film, the first thing they said was, "All right, we're going to pay you back! We've got some questions about *The Hobbit* that we're going to quiz *you* on!"'

LEFT & OPPOSITE: **Ryan Gage as the Master of Lake-town's valet, waiter, bookkeeper and general dogsbody, Alfrid.**

One of those questions might have been 'Who is Drogo Baggins?', for that was the part Ryan was offered. To be fair, the answer would not have been found in the pages of *The Hobbit*, but in the opening chapter of *The Fellowship of the Ring* where the patrons of *The Ivy Bush* are discussing Frodo's ancestry. 'His father was a Baggins,' Gaffer Gamgee tells his cronies. 'A decent respectable hobbit was Mr Drogo Baggins; there was never much to tell of him, till he was drownded.'

The tragic death of Drogo Baggins (resulting in Frodo being orphaned and adopted by Bilbo) was, for a time, featured as part of the prologue in the script. But Drogo, it seems, had been written into the story in order to find a role for the young actor who had made such an impression on the producers; when the scenes featuring Drogo were later abandoned, Ryan found himself being reconsidered for Alfrid, the role for which he had originally auditioned.

'I don't know how these things work,' admits Ryan, 'but they often have a few people that they like and then mix 'n' match the actors to the parts. Or, maybe they suddenly woke up one day and said: "Hold on! No, this is crazy! We should get Ryan to play Alfrid!" Anyway, that's the world I'm going to believe in!'

Describing Alfrid, Ryan is in no doubt that the character is not an entirely savoury individual: 'The first thing you have to say about him is that although he's not as evil as some characters – not exactly in league with the Orcs – he is vile; really and truly horrible. He's not *awful*-awful, but he's definitely a baddie and there are moments when he makes some terrible suggestions.'

Ryan breaks off and then adds with a laugh, 'But this is the sad bit: I think he probably had a really difficult beginning in life: probably an orphan, possibly born in a brothel; having a terrible childhood being bullied, beaten, and spat on in the great Dickensian tradition of little boys and all of that has twisted him. But he's a survivor and I feel sorry for him because – despite a fair amount of stupidity – he does have some intelligence. More than anything, he wants to be taken seriously but he isn't; people look down on him and, as a result, he's deeply resentful.'

Ryan pauses to question whether he is being too generous in his assessment of Alfrid's character: 'Maybe I'm just being kind to him, because I like him. I like the bits that he hates about himself: that sometimes his vanity betrays him and his ego spirals out of control with no relevance to the situation he's in; that he's kind of silly, but doesn't want to be; and that he can be quite brainless while thinking he's being terribly clever, something with which I can identify!'

Getting into the role, Ryan's portrayal underwent a change, he says, from his original audition at which he had played Alfrid 'rather like a used car salesman'. Putting on the costume gave him a different perspective, and a whole new physicality began to emerge for the character, based on the idea that the dank atmosphere of Lake-town has somehow infected his body: 'I came up with the idea that he's stiff and warped and hunched-up, almost as if his bones have become damp and mouldy due to the fact that he hasn't had enough sunlight. He can't lift his arm too high because he doesn't have much in the way of muscles and the sinews are sort of twisted. He can't move his neck much either – like when you wake up in the morning and you've got a crick in the neck and it's sore.'

Completing the look was the make-up: a monobrow (a

'He's not awful-*awful, but he's definitely a baddie and there are moments when he makes some terrible suggestions.'*

single eyebrow sitting above both eyes), a nasty outbreak of acne and some unpleasant-looking teeth. 'They are my teeth, but painted with several layers of different-coloured makeup. A lot of people came up to me to ask if the false teeth were uncomfortable, and I'd have to laugh. Anyway, the overall look is truly repellent.'

When it comes to talking about Alfrid's employer, Ryan doesn't hold back: 'The Master is horrible but, at the same time, he's very humorous and almost lovable. He's an extremely flatulent, fatuous, buffoonish, vain old toad of a man who is mean and selfish, who likes lording it over his people and treats Alfrid like dirt. Our first scene together was Alfrid emptying his droppings out of the window. But please note, there's no scene of Alfrid sanitizing his hands before presenting the Master with his breakfast – which, I thought, was a little victory for Alfrid!'

Describing their relationship, Ryan sees it as being driven by expediency: 'Alfrid doesn't really care for the Master, there's no real love lost there, but he's loyal because it suits his needs and, like many of the servant class, he needs someone to serve. What they have in common, however, is a shared joy in getting one over on people and feeling like they've used their cunning to manipulate a situation in their favour. The two of them are caught up in an old tradition; they're unique characters, but they're also archetypes who can be traced back to the Greek plays. The Master and Alfrid are a clever – but also slightly stupid – twosome, rather like Don Quixote and Sancho Panza.'

Ryan may have a jaundiced view of the Master, but when it comes to his perspective on the actor playing the role, he is boundless in his adulation: 'Stephen Fry is *amazing*: utterly lovely, charming and great fun to be around, although a nightmare to be on set with because he would tell me some of the filthiest jokes I've ever heard!'

Stephen is well known for his encyclopedic general knowledge, regularly displayed as chairman of the popular TV show, *QI*, something that Ryan was to personally discover when sharing a make-up room and a film set with him: 'I have, literally, experienced his entire knowledge base – there is not a subject I haven't heard him speak about! He's extraordinary! I'd just listen and try to absorb it all. You can guide him a little; for example, you can say, "Tell me about the history of Renaissance Europe or the mathematics of Pythagoras," and he will proceed to do just that. As a sort of naughty, but fun, game, I enjoyed trying to find questions to which he didn't have the answers. But it was very rare for him not to know something. His memory is phenomenal.'

For Ryan, Alfrid is very much a product of the place and age in which he finds himself: 'He's doing his best: he

wants to get by and has a desire to get on, but he's living in a difficult world, clawing himself higher and higher in a realm where there's nowhere to go. He's got to the very top of his tree in Lake-town and that's not exactly like working in the West Wing! He likes being close to power, but he hasn't the confidence to be powerful by himself. Alfrid is so terrified of the world that if he ever got into a real position of power he'd be totally paranoid.'

Perhaps the real secret to the character lies in his full name, something that Ryan only discovered after filming had begun: 'In my head, I'd been calling him "Smith" – Alfrid Smith – just so that he had a surname. Then one day, about halfway through, I got a re-write of a scene in which he's called Alfrid *Lickspittle*! It's such a good name – and so much better than "Smith" – because it suits a character who is so cunning and obsequious.'

Looking ahead to how Alfrid's future might unfold as a result of the coming of Thorin, Bilbo and Company, Ryan sees him as possibly behaving with the pragmatism typical of a civil servant: 'Governments come and go, but the civil servants are always there ready to serve somebody, anybody; switching allegiances and saying, "Yes, sir," to whoever's next in power. Alfrid is driven by survival and, when power shifts, his survival mechanism is simply to turn and smile at someone else...'

Paul Gray, Props Making Supervisor

BEDKNOBS & BROOMSTICKS

'THERE ARE NOT A LOT OF OFF-THE-RACK THINGS THAT YOU CAN GET FOR MIDDLE-EARTH!' THAT IS THE UNDERSTANDABLE VERDICT OF PAUL GRAY, PROPS MAKING SUPERVISOR.

If you look up the meaning of the word 'prop', you'll find three definitions, one of which is: 'An object other than furniture or costumes used on the set of a play or movie.' In a film such as *The Hobbit*, props tend to come in all shapes and sizes: 'Just about anything,' says Paul, 'from an item that you can hold in your hand, to something you'd have to move with a forklift truck!'

The number of props created for *The Hobbit* is legion, somewhere in the region – if anyone had time to count them – of 15,000 pieces, involving dozens of specialist craftspeople, among them potters, metalworkers, leatherworkers, armourers, jewellers, saddlers and boat-builders: 'Our backgrounds vary quite a lot,' says Paul: 'some come from strictly trade backgrounds, some from a particular craft, while others have gone through art school

and construction. This means that we are able to take the best skills from all those disciplines and apply them to whatever problem is at hand, and that's really the key to good prop making: people with an eye for the aesthetics and a knowledge of processes.'

What is particular about the approach to prop making on *The Hobbit* (as it was on *The Lord of the Rings*) is a commitment to authenticity: 'In the past, prop making has often been thought of as being about people with superglue, tape and balsa wood, and sometimes that might be what's required, but my approach with our workshop was that you need certain tools to do certain jobs, and we wanted to make them in as real a way as we possibly could. It's a better, more honest, approach, because we produce higher quality items and, in some cases, it actually takes less time to produce the

BELOW: **Bilbo's study, which contains dozens of props, all of which had to be individually crafted, painted and finished before being carefully included by the set decorators** (*left*). **The remarkable attention to detail is evidenced in the verisimilitude of this door to Beorn's house** (*right*). OPPOSITE: **Gollum's coracle is built using the remains of his victims** (*top*). **John Howe, Alan Lee and Peter Jackson aboard the full-scale prop of the Master's barge** (*bottom*).

real object well than to make what would essentially be a model of it. A cheaply made prop only needs to fail once on set to become really costly in terms of the dozens of expensive people who will be standing around killing time and costing the production money while whatever went wrong gets fixed. Better to make it the very best it can be to begin with.'

The range of props is as diverse as the day-to-day lives of the various peoples of Middle-earth: doorknobs for hobbit-holes in Hobbiton, silverware for Rivendell, outsized tools for Beorn, horse-drawn carts for the Elves of Mirkwood, fish-motif pottery for Lake-town, a carousel for Dale before the coming of the Dragon and charred objects for later scenes in the devastated city. Each new location in the story presented a unique challenge: 'Take Goblin-chain,' says Paul. 'Unfortunately, this is not something you can buy in the local chain-store! If I had to describe the Goblin aesthetic it would be that of a drunken madman: rough and ready, functional but cobbled together with little skill out of whatever detritus is at hand. So, because the links in Goblin-chain are large and crude looking, we had to cast it in sections and link it together.'

Props may often have a reference point in our world while, at the same time, having some aspect to their design or construction that is uniquely Middle-earthly. One such example would be Gollum's coracle. 'It is,' says Paul, 'a small one-man boat in the ancient style traditionally used in parts of Wales, Scotland and Ireland. The significant difference, however, is that Gollum's coracle happens to made out of the skin and bones of his Goblin victims!'

Limited availability of Goblin body-parts meant that the prop department had to simulate those gruesome materials as well as making it possible for Gollum to use it in order to paddle across his underground lake. Gollum's cave also required remnants of Goblin carcasses and scatterings of half-eaten fish and bits of bone. What do you make a half-eaten fish out of? 'As with all props,' explains Paul, 'it depends how it is to be used: if it just needs to be cheap and mountains of it are needed, we use foam, but if a prop needs to be durable then we make it out of urethane. If it needs to be safe so it can be safely stepped on – like fish on a cave floor – we use rubber.'

Apart from Gollum's 'fisheses', vast quantities of fish were also required for Lake-town: 'Everything we did reflected each character's environment and what they did

for a living. The people of Lake-town weren't meant to be wealthy people but fishermen, so we had a lot of fish: fresh-caught fish, drying fish, filleted fish and soft rubbery fish by the bucket-load.'

As a community built on water, Lake-town presented other challenges such as the need for lots of rope with authentic knots. 'Things have been made the way they have for centuries,' says Paul, 'for a very good reason – they work! Ropes and knots require a specialized skill and our job is to learn how to do that; we were lucky in that Production Designer, Dan Hennah, is an experienced sailor! Getting details correct is important, because if moviegoers see something that isn't quite right they'll pick up on it – either because they know what it should look like or, sometimes, just subliminally – and it detracts from the whole experience. So we focus on trying to do everything in a traditional way because it really adds to the authenticity of the scenes.'

Although far from prosperous, Lake-town is not without its riches – though most have been sequestered by the self-serving Master! In addition to hand-blown glass lamps, the Master's chamber boasts a library of volumes produced by the prop-making department: 'The weight of books and the problem of moving them around is a major consideration, so we had to find an alternative. In what

is a typical example of how the various departments on the film collaborate, Set Decorating produced the books, which we then cast in urethane; after that, Set Decorating added labelling and the Prop Painters enhanced them with gilding.'

No group of characters required more work than the Dwarves. 'The thing about Dwarves is that they are sort of 'Middle-earth bikers': hairy guys with beards, smoking and riding horses. What helped us establish the Dwarf aesthetic early on were the personal knives that we made for them and which reflected their work as metalsmiths.'

A number of other personal props were made for individual Dwarves, such as Ori's travelling writing implements, Bombur's ladle (multi-purpose cooking utensil and

Top: Lake-town net-menders display the skills of Production Designer, Dan Hennah. Below: Skilled metalworkers in the process of casting goblets that will end up as part of Smaug's hoard.

weapon) and various amusements designed for Bifur the toymaker: 'One I call the Whack-a-Dwarf was a toy that, when you crank it, a large Troll with a club tries to hit a Dwarf who dodges the blows. Another is an automaton of an Eagle in wood and copper that moves its head and beats its wings up and down.'

Less entertaining perhaps (or, possibly, more so) was the ear-trumpet used by the hard-of-hearing Oin. 'This is a particularly good example of a prop where we made many different versions – more than a dozen – for various scenes. The leading or, as we call it, "hero" prop was made out of brass, wood and leather, from which we took a mould so as to be able to make copies. We also made a crushable version lined with lead so it could be trodden on and then put back into shape again.'

Producing multiple copies is one of the banes of the prop-maker's life. 'Because of the differences in scale, if you see a Dwarf running along with a backpack that backpack could be the size worn by the actor or the size worn by the small-scale double: which has to look exactly the

same, but smaller. Multiply that by thirteen Dwarves and then, because there's a second unit that could be filming at the same time elsewhere, you can double that figure; then add in special variations such as lightweight, non-functioning versions and you begin to see just what a major undertaking backpacks are before you add on all their personal effects: knives, shovels, cooking pots, bed-rolls and so forth.'

As with every aspect of production, matters of scale are a constant challenge, as Paul admits: 'There are guidelines and it's all down to mathematical calculations, but some of the products we use are only available in certain sizes. So, for example, you may want to purchase fourteen-millimetre thickness metal in order to make something in wrought iron, but have to choose between sixteen- or

TOP: Samples of the hand-blown glass produced to the unique Lake-town aesthetic (*left*). The 'Whack-a-Dwarf' toy produced by Bifur as part of the Dwarves' moneymaking enterprise (*right*). LEFT: One of Oin's twelve ear-trumpet props was made of lead so that it could be squashed and put back into shape.

ABOVE: **Bilbo's crockery was needed in plentiful supply considering how much would be intentionally broken during filming by his 'party guests'.** BELOW: **The toy dragon kite first seen in the sky over Dale.** OPPOSITE: **The fully working, full-size ballista built for a flashback scene at Dale (*top*). The workbench of Leading Hand: Leather Tack, Tim Abbot, just one member of the vast army of artisans who brought Middle-earth to life (*bottom*).**

twelve-millimetre because that's how it comes. It's at that point that you just have to cheat the sums!'

Another factor to impact on the design of a prop is whether it is to be used in a scene where stunts are involved, such as the treatment Bilbo's crockery in Bag End (all specially made by the Props Department's resident potter) receives at the hands of the Dwarves: 'We had half-baked versions of the plates that could be thrown and smashed and we cast other versions made out of soft rubber, that they could be bounced and juggled.'

How a stunt prop is made depends on whether it needs to be light or flexible or whether it's necessary to protect the actor, the prop or both. As an example, Paul talks about the varieties of staff that might be required for Bilbo, Gandalf and others: 'There is the "hero", the most beautiful staff, which, in order to achieve a nice level of finish, has to have weight to it. But if you've got the actor riding around on a horse with it, we'll do a soft, ultra-light version. It's also possible that the same staff might be used for fighting, in which case you have another durable version, because the stunt performers are going to pound each other into submission with it, and the staff needs to survive!'

A great deal of what gets created for the films goes unnoticed by audiences and on *The Hobbit* there were whole sequences that failed to make it into the final film, although many of the props not seen when *An Unexpected Journey* first premiered can now be enjoyed in the Extended Edition version of the film.

'We made a lot of things for the marketplace in Hobbiton,' recalls Paul, 'including a puppet show and a great deal of food – fruit, vegetables (and fish again) – that had to be cast in urethane because we were on the set too long to use real food. But perhaps the most exciting prop we made was the ballista, a huge crossbow used by Bard's ancestor, Girion, Lord of Dale, in an attempt to defend the city against the attack by Smaug. It was a fairly complex piece of gear to design around: a working crossbow with two pairs of two-metre long arms, able to rotate and pivot up and

THE OFFICIAL MOVIE GUIDE

down. It needed to be strong enough to be dramatically handled by the actor on set and look like it does what it's supposed to do when it's loaded and fired without endangering the actor or anyone else. It took a real pounding, but they got what they needed out of it and it ended up being really quite cool!'

If there's a word to sum up the work of the Props Department, it would be 'deadlines' – or, in *two* words, 'fast deadlines'! 'Yes,' says Paul, 'that's pretty much the name of the game! And that is why we set up the workshop in a way that allows us to be able to react on any given day to whatever demands come through the door. We always have all the materials we might use permanently in stock, because you can't wait until you hear that a prop is required *then* order the material, get it in, and make it. A prop has to be there when it's needed.'

Or even sooner, as was the case with Thror's key to the secret door in the Lonely Mountain. 'We had a design, and the scene in which it was to feature was scheduled for a week ahead, but then the schedule changed and it was suddenly needed by the following morning!

So our traditional process of sculpting, moulding and casting had to wait until later and the key as it first appeared on film was one that we had rapidly whittled out of a block of soft pewter! There were ten or so other versions after that, but knowing that we can meet such exacting deadlines is an achievement we're all proud of, along with knowing that, when we watch the movies, during practically every second of the film we are seeing something that was produced in our workshop.'

SPLENDOUR, LUST & GLORY

JED BROPHY, IN CHARACTER AS THE LIGHT-FINGERED NORI, DESCRIBES THE FILM SET FOR SMAUG'S LAIR: 'BRILLIANT! NOT SCARED OF DRAGONS! LOTS OF LOVELY GOLD! LOTS OF LOVELY STUFF FOR ME TO STEAL! LOVE IT!'

When J.R.R. Tolkien depicts Bilbo's first glimpse of the great Dwarven hall beneath the Lonely Mountain, he writes of the vastness of the wealth guarded by the sleeping Dragon: 'Beneath him… and about him on all sides stretching away across the unseen floors, lay countless piles of precious things, gold wrought and unwrought, gems and jewels, and silver red-stained in the ruddy light.' Bilbo, we are told, had heard stories of the wonder of Dragon-hoards but, says the author, he was totally unprepared for 'the splendour, the lust, the glory' of the sight that met his eyes.

The challenge of putting such a scene on film was not limited to creating an appropriately terrifying fire-breathing Dragon; it also required the amassing of sufficient gold, silver, treasure and precious artefacts to represent Smaug's vast accumulated wealth.

The far reaches of the gilded landscape in which Bilbo first meets Smaug would eventually be created digitally in post-production, but a good few treasure chest-loads of authentic-looking loot was still needed for when characters find themselves in the midst of the plunder.

'What we really had to deal with was volume,' says Props Making Supervisor, Paul Gray. 'We needed to create layers of detail and we started with what we called "treasure blankets". We built a generic-looking pile of jewelled

cups, swords, coins and bullion and then moulded that and created one-metre-square blankets that could be cut and assembled as underlying texture. After that we cast real cups that had a more metallic sheen to them and that provided another layer that went on top; then we had other things – our "hero props" as we refer to them – that were meant to be seen in the foreground, as the camera was panning by, including a great many gold coins.'

Talk of coins brings back the memory of a conversation from some months before Smaug's hoard was scheduled for filming. Prop Master, Nick Weir, described one of several challenges he was facing as we sat having a cup of coffee in the Art Department at Wellington's Stone Street Studios: 'If we wanted to cover the top of this coffee table with a heap of coins,' he said, it would take several thousand, so we have to face the fact that there's a tidal wave of coinage coming our way!'

THIS PAGE, OPPOSITE & OVERLEAF: **Almost 300,000 coins were cast in five different designs before being plated in copper and brass (*above*) but for those special items seen in close-up (*right*) they had to be plated in gold to simulate real treasure. Yet even this huge amount barely filled one of the emormous soundstages that Martin Freeman as Bilbo would attempt to traverse.**

Set Director, Ra Vincent, takes up the story: 'Smaug's treasure was a numbers game, where we had specific quantities that had to be achieved in order to fill the environment whilst at the same time keeping within the budget.'

In the event, six tons of aluminium was ordered, from which 290,000 coins were minted in five different designs and plated with a mixture of copper and brass. They may have been good enough for long shots and background dressing, but it was a different story when it came to coins that would be seen in close-up, as Ra explains: 'The funny thing about gold is you can only achieve an authentic look by using *real* gold. There is really no way to fake it, as we discovered when we went to a foundry and cast in excess of two thousand bronze coins that were then plated with eighteen- or twenty four-carat gold to a level of super shininess. It was a highly labour-intensive job and it turned

out that even this relatively small quantity added up to an awful lot of gold.'

Yet who knows the true extent of a Dragon's hoard? 'From the start,' says Paul Gray, 'we always knew that whatever we made, it would never be enough. And true to expectations, however much we produced, they always wanted more!'

And so, in addition to the avalanche of gold coins, there was a treasure trove of 1,200 one-of-a-kind goblets, over half of which were individually embellished by hand with faux gems and precious stones. Filming on HFR (High Frame Rate) cameras, says Ra, means that nothing can be left to chance:

'We have created thousands of seemingly background objects, but everyone knew that the chances of them remaining in the background were a myth! Shooting in high definition means there's not a detail that goes unnoticed. At the conceptual stage, our emphasis is always on quality of product and it's really worked to our benefit in that every handmade piece in Smaug's collection is finished to the nth degree.'

Truly, a hoard worthy of a Dragon's lust, but not, it should be noted, acquired without cost. For in creating Smaug's lair the filmmakers bought up every single last can and pot of gold paint throughout the entire length and breadth of New Zealand!

SMAUG, THE CHIEFEST AND GREATEST OF CALAMITIES

A CCORDING TO J.R.R. TOLKIEN, SMAUG WAS 'A MOST SPECIALLY GREEDY, STRONG AND WICKED' DRAGON AND HIS NOTORIETY AS A HARBINGER OF DEATH AND DESTRUCTION IS KNOWN THROUGHOUT MIDDLE-EARTH.

'Smaug the Terrible,' says Bofur, in *The Hobbit: An Unexpected Journey*, 'chiefest and greatest calamity of our age. Airborne fire-breather, teeth like razors, claws like meat hooks, extremely fond of precious metals... He'll melt the flesh off your bones in the blink of an eye! Think furnace with wings. Flash of light, searing pain, then – *poof!* – you're nothing more than a pile of ash!'

Bringing such a monstrously fearful creature to life on screen is clearly a challenge, especially when so many artists and illustrators have graphically depicted him over the years, beginning with the book's author and culminating in the team at Weta Digital, whose work will see him realized in three-dimensional glory.

Our first glimpses of Smaug in the opening of *An Unexpected Journey*, as he blazes a path of destruction through Dale and bursts into the kingdom of Erebor under the Lonely Mountain, are limited to a rushing shadow, a volcanic eruption of fire and the merest glimpse of talon,

wing and tail. 'Smaug's attack on Erebor,' says Concept Artist John Howe, 'has all the hallmarks of a natural disaster, something totally unstoppable: an avalanche, a forest fire, or a flood in the shape of this huge scaly Dragon.'

After little more than the blink of a Dragon's eye at the climax of the first film, audiences eagerly anticipate seeing the rest of him in *The Desolation of Smaug*. As Lindsey Crummett of the Design Department at Weta Workshop puts it: 'Smaug is the "rock star" of *The Hobbit* – the equivalent to Gollum in *The Lord of the Rings* – so he's the character that everybody can't wait to see.'

Weta Workshop Creature and Character Designer, Andrew Baker, agrees: 'The end of *The Hobbit* is one of the coolest parts of the book and one of the biggest and most exciting characters in those chapters is obviously Smaug. That makes him the biggest reveal in the trilogy.'

As you might suspect, Andrew and colleagues are not pre-empting that moment of revelation: 'The design process,' he says, 'is a lengthy one, because it is about trying new concepts and continuing to push ideas around.'

Those concepts and ideas have been tried out and pushed around for some while, in fact dating back to the earliest days of pre-production, as Concept Designer, Ben Mauro, explains: 'Richard Taylor asked us to come up with the widest possible range of ideas: everything from classical Dragon imagery to visualizations that were less conventional.'

Fresh explorations followed when Peter Jackson took up the directorial reins, this time increasingly in pursuit of a creature that, whilst being monstrously larger-than-life, was – in terms of the filmic world of Middle-earth

OPPOSITE: **Smaug blasts through the Front Gate of Erebor.** ABOVE: **The Dragon awakes!** BELOW: **With head-camera and microphone in place, Benedict Cumberbatch unleashes the power of his inner Dragon.**

– more 'realistic'. 'Many of the creature designers,' says Lindsey, 'will start with where that creature lives and how its anatomy might be dictated by its habitat; so, in the case of Smaug, the fact that he lives in mountain caverns, deep underground will impact on his appearance.'

'The fact that he has lived in the Lonely Mountain for hundreds of years,' adds Andrew, 'meant that we wanted to create an ancient creature whose long history was etched into its features.'

A vast art gallery of concepts, ranging from paintings via pencil drawings to rapid sketches have been refined into an idea of 'Dragon-ness' that is then visualized as a physical or digital sculpture so that the director and the animators can explore detailing such as skin texture and the way in which the creature will move. Only then does Weta Digital start work on the animation that will bring the Dragon to life on screen.'

Reflecting on the nature of the beast whose fiery shadow hangs over *The Hobbit* trilogy, John Howe says: 'He is ancient, he is vain and he is very, very evil. He flies and he breathes fire, so he has all the amazing graphic elements you'd want in a Dragon, and he carries with him the weight of all our memories of every Dragon that's ever been invented since humankind's earliest tales, myths and legends. Smaug the Golden is the last of the Dragons in Middle-earth, a symbol of something that is vanishing from that world and a closing chapter in the history of Dragons.'

Benedict Cumberbatch

A CONVERSATION WITH SMAUG

'WHAT ARE SMAUG'S STRENGTHS?' BENEDICT CUMBERBATCH IS CATALOGUING THE ATTRIBUTES OF THE FEARSOME CHARACTER THAT HE PLAYS IN *THE HOBBIT*. 'WELL, HE IS ANCIENT, ENORMOUS AND POWERFUL, BREATHES FIRE, CAN FLY AND IS INCREDIBLY QUICK FOR SOMETHING OF THAT SIZE AND SCALE.'

Quoting Tolkien, the actor reflects on Smaug's boast that his armoured skin is like tenfold shields, his claws are like spears, his teeth swords, his wings a hurricane, his tail is a thunderbolt and his breath — *death*. 'Smaug,' he says, 'is a solo army: everything you'd ever need in a battle to win it. He is an utter, destructive force of nature.'

So much for Smaug's strengths, what of his weaknesses? 'Really,' says Benedict, 'it's his emotional state that makes him vulnerable: his pride and his arrogance. And that arrogance is actually one of the reasons that I got this part; they said: "That guy's an arrogant ******, let's give him the role of Smaug!"'

Whilst that is *not* the real reason why Benedict secured the role, it is true that he has played his fair share of arrogant characters, most notably the title role in the BBC television series, *Sherlock*, in which he co-starred with the future Mr Baggins, Martin Freeman.

Having studied drama at the University of Manchester and trained as an actor at the London Academy of Music and Dramatic Art, Benedict appeared on stage in classical roles as well as getting noticed in various TV series, among them *Cambridge Spies*, *Fortysomething* and *Dunkirk*. In 2004 he received a BAFTA nomination for his acclaimed performance in *Hawking*, a television drama based on the early career of Stephen Hawking, the cosmologist who would succumb to motor neuron disease. Other biographical portrayals on the large and small screen include the nineteenth-century British Prime Minister, William Pitt the Younger, painter Vincent Van Gogh and Soviet spy, Guy Burgess.

In 2010, Benedict achieved international fame as a modern-day incarnation of Arthur Conan Doyle's famous investigating detective, Sherlock Holmes, in the hugely successful series, *Sherlock*. The following year, he starred in the

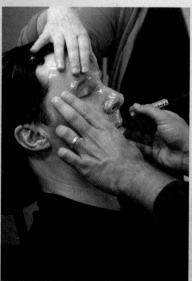

LEFT: Benedict Cumberbatch is made ready for the motion capture camera; precisely marking his face using a mask ensures that every nuance of his performance is picked up. ABOVE: Bilbo goes for gold as he warily wades through treasure towards a conversation with Smaug. BELOW: Benedict makes every effort to be the best-dressed character on the set when he meets Bilbo and friends.

National Theatre production of *Frankenstein*, alternating with Johnny Lee Miller in the roles of the Creature and his eponymous creator, in addition to appearing in the films *Tinker, Tailor, Soldier, Spy* and *War Horse*.

Hearing that casting was beginning for *The Hobbit*, Benedict went for an audition with Hubbard Casting in London, the agency that featured prominently in putting together the cast of *The Lord of the Rings*. Like many other British actors, Benedict recorded a video audition to be sent to Peter Jackson, Fran Walsh and Philippa Boyens in New Zealand.

Benedict expressed a desire to audition for the voice of Smaug, motivated by his own childhood introduction to Tolkien's story that had come from having the book read to him by his father. 'It was,' the actor says, 'the first book I ever had in my head as an imaginary world and it was a really rich part of the tapestry of my

upbringing, not because I read it off the page, but because it was passed on to me orally, brought to imaginative reality by my father.'

Actor Timothy Carlton had read *The Hobbit* to his young son in episodes. 'He brought this already rich, magical world to life for me,' Benedict remembers. 'My dad

MAKING A
DRAGON ROAR

*Sound Designer, David Farmer,
describes how Smaug acquired his
snarls and bellows.*

'Smaug on the rampage is very scary. His vocals when he is attacking can be divided into two categories: the attack roars themselves and vocal elements added to his fireballs to give them a more emotive quality.

'People may be surprised to know that Smaug's attack roars are mostly made up from the roars of a very large pig that I recorded one morning while they were complaining about waiting to be fed! Quite by accident, some of Smaug's other roars came from an equally unexpected source – my daughter! I had done a Career Day demonstration at her school, where I showed first-grade students how I could turn my daughter's voice into — yes, a Dragon! At the time I had no intention of actually using that sound anywhere in the film, but while I was searching around for material to make more Smaug sounds I came across my daughter's 'Dragon' roar. I really didn't expect it to work, but it fitted perfectly, ramping up the sound of the pig roars and adding exactly the dimension I was after.

'When we're one-to-one with Smaug, his vocals – less of a roar and more guttural and growly – are provided by alligators. I had heard, and sparingly used, alligator growls before, though always as a layered element to add size to some creature or other and, throughout my career, had been hoping for an opportunity to record the reptiles. I think the powers-that-be had been holding out on me, since I finally got to record some alligators in Florida in the same year that I began working on *The Hobbit*. The last sound of *An Unexpected Journey*, when Smaug opens his eye, is six alligator growls layered together.'

is an extraordinary actor, so he did all the voices: he was brilliant as the Dwarves, very gruff, stocky and earnest; his Bilbo was more free and skittish, but also grounded and homely. But what I chiefly remember was his Smaug, because he did a very good Dragon with an amazing gravelly, growling voice.'

Casting Director, Dan Hubbard, suggested that Benedict should audition off-camera – in sound only – so that the producers would be able to focus on the vocal performance without being influenced by the actor's youthful appearance. Benedict recalls: 'How can he possibly play a Dragon? He looks like a puppy and, as someone once said of me, has a face like a horse! So, yes, it's impossible to imagine me having a centuries-old voice. But I'm an actor and we don't have centuries-old actors, so you just have to distance yourself from the enormity of expectation because, if you start playing with expectation, you're playing with fire: it's damning, distracting and destructive.'

Undaunted (but unseen), the actor nevertheless tried to embody a sense of physicality into his reading: 'Just a few subtle head movements, getting the shoulders working a bit and some serpentine stuff with my neck. I really had a very strong idea of how Smaug looked, what he felt and how he moved.'

As for the vocal performance, however, there was only one source of inspiration: recollections of his father's bedtime readings. When, about a year later, Benedict received the news that he would be providing the voice for one of literature's most famous Dragons and finally met Peter Jackson face to face, he took his future director somewhat by surprise with a disarming confession: 'I told him, "I'm really going to be giving a second-hand performance as Smaug, because, basically, I ripped it off from my dad!"'

Benedict recalls breaking the news to his father that he had captured a plum role in *The Hobbit*: 'It was a very satisfying day in my life as an actor to be able to go home and say to my dad, "I'm playing Smaug, and I've got you to thank for it!" I really do owe him a lot.' He pauses and then adds: 'He's getting a cut!'

Benedict's audition had so impressed the filmmakers that, as with Andy Serkis' interpretation of Gollum, his portrayal of Smaug would expand to encompass a physical as well as vocal performance: 'I had been determined to include movement in my audition and so was thrilled when I was asked by Peter to do MoCap, as well as voice, to help influence the animation process.'

Before flying to New Zealand, Benedict decided to undertake some authentic animal research: 'I did the typical actorly thing and visited London Zoo and went to the reptile house to spend time watching snakes and lizards.' As

Benedict discovered, quite a lot of reptile activity involves an *absence* of activity: 'I began to understand that, as a predator, Smaug is both all-powerful and completely still – at least until he is awoken. I also decided that his voice should have only the slightest vocalization, almost as if it is lazily breathed out of him.'

All these observations played into the motion-capture performance that Benedict gave as part of the preparation for creating the CGI Dragon. Dressed in a figure-hugging Lycra suit, and with his face covered in dots 'like ritualistic tribal markings', he set to work being Smaug. 'It's a proper old challenge, imagining yourself into a vast creature in a huge space when in reality you're crawling around on a bit of grey carpet. At the beginning of the day, Peter and I looked at one another and I said, "I don't know what I'm going to do. Shall I just go out there and do stuff that I have in my head?" And he said, "Yeah, just give it a go. Just do it." So, I did a lot of roaring and scampering about and Peter gave me notes: "Don't be too angry here, save it… Try a bit more vindication… Don't forget that you're playing a game with Bilbo." It was exhausting but a great day.'

As part of his search to find the Dragon within him, Benedict recorded his dialogue lying on his belly. 'There aren't many snakes that have legs to stand up on, so I thought that this was the place to start from if I was going to inhabit it physically.'

One of the most memorable scenes in the book is Bilbo's invisible, Ring-wearing conversation with Smaug that involves almost as many riddles as his earlier encounter with Gollum. As Benedict explains: 'Smaug can't see this person that he knows is in his space, but he can smell him, hear his breathing, feel his air. The Dragon's senses are highly attuned; he's a hunter and there's a mouse in the cat's lair – something for him to have fun with. He's intrigued and there's an element of game-playing, which immediately kicks off the riddling.'

For Benedict, comparisons can be drawn between the Dragon's greediness and a major theme found in Tolkien's later work. 'There's a parallel between *The Hobbit* and *The Lord of the Rings*: that of the corrupting lust for power. Smaug is a symbol of that – a sleepy serpent atop his pile of gold. His possessiveness is sad and pathetic. Everyone thinks of Dragons as powerful and majestic, awesome and inspiring. But this Dragon is simply corrupt. His hoard does nothing for him, he's living on it, but he can't take it with him. There's an old saying, "There are no pockets in a shroud". And there are none on a Dragon either!'

BELOW: The celebration of Smaug: Peter Jackson and his Company of actors welcome newcomer Benedict Cumberbatch into their midst.

Epilogue:

EAST IS EAST...

'**O**UT OF THIS COLOURFUL CAST OF CHARACTERS, DWARVES, ELVES, ORCS, WIZARDS AND DRAGONS, BILBO – EVEN THOUGH HE'S JUST A HOBBIT – IS, I THINK, THE ONE WE RELATE TO MOST CLOSELY.' PETER JACKSON IS TALKING ABOUT THE QUALITIES OF *THE HOBBIT*'S CENTRAL CHARACTER. 'WHAT'S IMPORTANT ABOUT A STORY LIKE THIS IS THAT THERE'S SOMEONE INVOLVED WITH WHOM WE CAN EMPATHIZE.'

At large in a world of heroes and warriors, Bilbo Baggins – is 'everyman', an ordinary (yet, in some ways, extraordinary) representative of 'us', the reader of Tolkien's book, the viewer of Jackson's films.

'Bilbo is a critical character,' says Peter, 'because we get to live out the story and experience the movie through his eyes and, quite a lot of the time, he is feeling nervous and uncomfortable, never having seen monsters before, never having been in a battle, yet stuck in the middle of this dangerous adventure. That makes him someone about whom we think, "Oh, yeah, that's precisely how *I* would be reacting! If I encountered a Troll or an Orc or a Dragon, I'd be doing exactly that!" We know that we wouldn't be grabbing swords and getting stuck into a fight like the other characters, we'd be doing what Bilbo does – looking anxious and awkward and secretly wishing we were safely back home.'

Indeed, on more than one occasion, J.R.R. Tolkien has his book's title-character wistfully reflect on how much he would prefer to be back, safe and sound, in his cosy hobbit-hole, just as, in *The Desolation of Smaug*, Bilbo grumpily points out to the Dwarves and Bard on the way to Lake-town: 'I should never have left Bag End, that was my first mistake. You know, we have a saying in The Shire; we learn it from birth: "You never venture *East*!"'

But it's too late now: East is East, Bilbo is there and the adventure is far from over...

ACKNOWLEDGEMENTS

This book would have not been possible without the enthusiastic cooperation of everyone – cast and crew – involved in the making of *The Hobbit*. You will come across the names of a number of the following in the pages of this book; others found their way into my last book and some will make it into the next, but I am acknowledging them all here, with admiration for their work and grateful appreciation for making my task as chronicler, newshound and tittle-tattler so enlightening and agreeable:

Gino Acevedo, Matt Aitken, Judy Alley, Richard Armitage, Andrew Baker, John Bell, Jarl Benzon, Cate Blanchett, Orlando Bloom, Richard Bluck, Melissa Booth, Chris Boswell, Glenn Boswell, Philippa Boyens, Simon Bright, Jed Brophy, Adam Brown, Hamish Brown, Bob Buck, Andy Buckley, John Callen, Guy Campbell, Róisín Carty, Sophie Collie, Paula Collier, Jared Connon, Lindsey Crummett, Benedict Cumberbatch, Carolynne Cunningham, Colin Davidson, Matt Dravitzki, Luke Evans, David Farmer, Caro Fenton, Karen Flett, Robyn Forster, Beverly Francis, Martin Freeman, Stephen Fry, Alex Funke, Mark Gabites, Ryan Gage, Sam Genet, Paul Gray, Mark Hadlow, Peter Hambleton, Chris Hennah, Dan Hennah, Amelia Hemphill, Belindalee Hope, John Howe, Barry Humphries, Stephen Hunter, Peter Jackson, Tony Johnson, Sean Kelly, Peter Swords King, Adam Kinsman, William Kircher, Tami Lane, Jennifer Langford, Jamie Lawrence, Pauline Laws, Alan Lee, Andrew Lesnie, Joe Letteri, Sophie Lewis-Smith, Evangeline Lilly, Deborah Logan, Simon Lowe, Letty MacPhedran, Paul Maples, Ann Maskrey, Brian Massey, Ben Mauro, Hayley May, Sylvester McCoy, Ian McKellen, Leith McPherson, Graham McTavish, Sebastian Meek, Amy Miller, Amy Minty, Eileen Moran, Liz Mullane, James Nesbitt, Peggy & Mary Nesbitt, Terry Notary, Dean O'Gorman, Steve Old, Jabez Olssen, Lee Pace, Rowan Panther, Mikael Persbrandt, Kasia Pol, Dallas Poll, Ceris Price, Paul Randall, Daniel Reeve, Miranda Rivers, Tania Rodger, Eric Saindon, Andy Serkis, Kiran Shah, Glenn Shaw, Ken Stott, Ri Streeter, Victoria Sullivan, Richard Taylor, Jack Tippler, Aidan Turner, Grace Ty-Wood, Ra Vincent, Fran Walsh, Hugo Weaving, Zane Weiner, Nick Weir, Dave Whitehead, Jamie Wilson, Elijah Wood, Amy Wright, Laurie Wright and Brigitte Yorke.

And at Warner Bros.: Elaine Piechowski, Victoria Selover, Melanie Swartz, Susannah Scott and Jill Benscoter.

I am much obliged to Michael Pellerin and Susan Lee for their unique insights; and to Debbie and Rhys Barlow, Michael Goldberg, Jane Johnson, Jonathan Kingsbury, Jack Machiela, Ryan Rasmussen, Michele Scullion, Michelle Sinnot and Jessica Yates for appreciated kindnesses and for the supply of useful information.

At HarperCollins*Publishers* my thanks go to Victoria Barnsley, Andrew Cunning, Kate Elton, Simon Johnson, Charles Light, Gareth Shannon, and all in the Rights and Sales teams.

I am specially indebted to David Brawn for the opportunity to pursue Bilbo's journey to the desolation of Smaug; to Terence Caven for another elegant design; and to my editor, Chris Smith, who manages to temper the role of taskmaster with liberal measures of encouragement and inspiration, not to mention wonderful good humour and astonishing levels of forbearance.

Finally, personal thanks go to Philip Patterson of Marjacq Scripts for his support; and to my partner, David Weeks, for enduring yet another expedition through the wilds and wastes of Middle-earth.

If you are interested in learning more about the filmmaking journey of *The Hobbit*, find out how it began in:

THE HOBBIT
AN UNEXPECTED JOURNEY
OFFICIAL MOVIE GUIDE

Packed with exclusive behind-the-scenes photographs, and featuring numerous exclusive interviews with the stars and filmmakers, this official illustrated guide by Brian Sibley tells the detailed story of the making of the first of Peter Jackson's trilogy of film adaptations.

ISBN 978 0 00 746446 3